It's Getting Later All the Time

Also by Antonio Tabucchi

Antonio Tabucchi

It's Getting Later All the Time

**A NOVEL IN THE FORM
OF LETTERS**

**Translated from the Italian
by Alastair McEwen**

A New Directions Book

Manufactured in the United States of America
New Directions Books are printed on acid-free paper.
First published as New Directions Paperbook 1042 in 2006
Published simultaneously in Canada by Penguin Books Canada Limited
Interior design by Sylvia Frezzolini Severance

Library of Congress Cataloging-in-Publication Data

Tabucchi, Antonio, 1943-
 [Si sta facendo sempre più tardi. English]
 It's getting later all the time : a novel in the form of letters / by
Antonio Tabucchi ; translated from the Italian by Alastair McEwen.
    p. cm.
 ISBN-13: 978-0-8112-1546-6
 ISBN-10: 0-8112-1546-6
 I. McEwen, Alastair. II. Title.
 PQ4880.A24S513 2006
 853'.914—dc22

                              2006007369

New Directions Books are published for James Laughlin
by New Directions Publishing Corporation
80 Eighth Avenue, New York 10011

FOURTH PRINTING

Contents

This book is dedicated to my friend Davide Benati who looks, understands and transforms into color.

Avanti, 'ndrè
avanti, 'ndrè
che bel divertimento.
Avanti, 'ndrè
avanti, 'ndrè
la vita è tutta qua.

(Back and forth
back and forth
what fun it is.
Back and forth
back and forth
that's life for you.)

(Refrain of an Italian popular song)

A Ticket in the
Middle of the Sea

My Dear,

I don't think the diameter of this island amounts to any more than thirty miles, at most. A narrow coast road runs all the way around it, often with sheer drops over the sea. But mostly it runs level along a barren coastline that slopes down to solitary little shingly beaches bordered with tamarisks parched by the salt, and occasionally I stop at some of these beaches. And is from one of these that I am talking to you, in a low voice, because the afternoon and the sea and this white light have made you close your eyelids, as you lie stretched out here beside me. I see your breast rising to the measured rhythm of the breathing of someone sleeping, and I don't want to wake you. Certain poets we know would really like this place, because it is so rugged and essential, with its rocks, barren hillocks, thorn-bushes, and goats. I have even come to think that this island doesn't exist, and I found it only because I imagined it. It's not a place, it's a hole: a hole in the net, I mean. These days there is a net in which you cannot avoid being captured, it seems, and it is a drag-net. I persist in looking for holes in this net. Now I almost seemed to hear your ironic little laugh: "Oh come on, here we go again!" But no: your eyelids are closed and you haven't moved. I only imagined it. I wonder what time it is? I am not wearing my watch, which is completely unnecessary here for that matter.

But I was describing this place to you. The first thing you think of, here, is the excessiveness of the excess of the times we live in, at least for those of us lucky enough to be on the good side of things. Instead, consider the goats: they get by on nothing, they eat even briar and they lick salt. The more I look at goats, the more I like them. On this beach there are seven or eight wandering among the stones, without a goatherd; they probably belong to the owners of the little house where I stopped at midday. There is a kind of café beneath a canopy made of reeds where you can eat olives, cheese, and melon. The old woman who served me is deaf and I had to yell to ask for these few things; she told me that her husband would come right away, but I didn't see her husband, perhaps he's a fantasy of hers, or maybe I misunderstood. She makes the cheese with her own hands; she took me into the courtyard of the house, a dusty open space full of thistles surrounded by a dry stone wall where the goat pen is. I made a scything gesture with my hand, as if to signify that she ought to cut the thistles that stick out and make you trip. She responded with a gesture that was identical, but more purposeful. Goodness knows what she meant by that hand slashing the air like a blade. Alongside the barns the farmhouse was extended by a kind of cellar carved out of the rock, where she makes her cheese, which is not much more than a salted ricotta seasoned in the dark, with a reddish crust of chili peppers. Her creamery is a room dug out of the rock, cool, freezing I'd say. There is a granite skimmer where she leaves the milk to curdle, and a vat for the whey, as well as a corrugated board set at an angle on which she kneads the curd as if it were clothing on a washboard, wringing it to get all the water out. After this she puts it into two molds in which it sets; these are wooden molds that snap open and shut; one is round and quite normal, while the other is shaped like the ace of spades, or at least that's how it looked to me, very much like the playing card suit. I bought a round cheese and I would have liked one like the ace of spades, but the old woman refused and I had to content myself with the round one. I asked her why but all I got in return was a series of guttural, graceless, almost strident growls accompanied by indecipherable gestures. She traced a circle around her belly and touched her heart. Who knows: perhaps it was meant to signify that that type of cheese was reserved solely for certain essential ceremonies of life: birth, death. But as I was telling you, maybe it's only my imagination at work, which often gallops off, as you know. In any event the cheese is exquisite between these two slices of black bread, which I am eating after having poured a little olive oil over it, of which there is no shortage around here, and a few leaves of the thyme used to season every dish, from fish to wild rabbit. I would have liked to ask you if you too were hungry. Look, it's exquisite, I told you, it's something unrepeatable, in a little while it too will have vanished in the net that is wrapping itself around us; there are no holes or escape routes for this cheese, this is your chance. But I didn't want to disturb you, your sleep was so beautiful, and so right, and I kept quiet. I saw a vessel pass by in the distance and I thought of the word I am writing to you: vessel. I saw a vessel pass by laden with . . . ? Guess.

I entered the sea very slowly, with a feeling of panic, as befits this place. As I was entering the water, with my senses predisposed to those things that the noonday sun and the azure and the sea salt and solitude arouse in a man, I heard your ironic little laugh from behind me. I preferred to ignore it and proceeded until the water was almost up to my navel, that idiotic girl is pretending to sleep, I thought, and she's making fun of me. As if out of defiance, I went forward and, still out of defiance, but also to mock you, I suddenly turned around, exhibiting my nakedness. Hey presto!, I cried. You didn't move an inch, but your voice came to me very clearly, especially the sardonic tone. Bravo, you're still in shape! congratulations, but Honey Beach was twenty years ago, and a lot of water has gone under the bridge since then, so watch out, maybe you've shot your bolt! Rather venomous words, you have to admit, aimed at someone going into the sea, playing the mature faun. I looked at myself, and I looked at the azure around me and never did a metaphor strike me as more apt, and I was seized by a sense of the ridiculous, and with it an amazement, like a disorientation, and a kind of shame, and so I brought my hands forward to cover myself, pointlessly, given that before me there was no one, only sea and sky and nothing else. And you were far away, motionless on the beach, too far away to have whispered those words to me. I'm hearing voices, I thought, it's an auditory hallucination. And for a moment I felt paralyzed, an ice-cold sweat broke out on my neck, and the water seemed like cement to me, as if I were trapped in it and would suffocate in it walled up for ever, like a fossil dragonfly trapped in a block of quartz. And with a struggle, step after step, without turning around, I tried to flee the panic that now really had me in its grip, that panic that makes you lose your bearings; I retreated as far as the beach where at least I knew that in any case you were there as a point of reference, that sure point of reference you've always been for me, stretched out on a towel alongside my own.

But I'm flying off at a tangent, as they say, because if I'm not mistaken I was talking to you about the island. So: if at a guess its diameter isn't more than thirty miles, according to me there's no more than one inhabitant for every four square miles. Hardly a soul, really. Perhaps there are more goats, in fact I'm positive there are. The only thing the earth produces, apart from the brambles and the prickly pears, are melons: where the stony ground becomes a yellowish sand, the inhabitants grow melons, only melons, small as grape-fruits and extremely sweet. The melon fields are divided up by clusters of grape vines that look almost wild and grow in holes dug in the sand, where the brine can't burn the plants and where the overnight dew collects, which must be their only nourishment. The grapes yield a very strong dark rosé;

I think it is the only drink on the island, apart from tisanes brewed from spontaneous herbs that are drunk in abundance, cold too, and are bitter but strongly scented. Some are yellow, made from a kind of thorny crocus that flourishes among the rocks and looks like a flat artichoke. This highly intoxicating drink, much stronger than wine, is reserved for the sick and the dying. First it brings an unusual sense of wellbeing and then it makes you sleep for a long time, and when you wake up you don't know how much time has passed: maybe a few days, and you don't dream at all.

I'm sure that you're thinking that in a place like this it would be necessary to bring a tent. Yes, but where to pitch it? Among the rocks?, among the melons? And besides, you know, I was never much at pitching tents, they came out all lopsided on me, poor things, you felt sorry for them. But I found a place in the village. It seems incredible, but when you arrive after a climb up a ramshackle stairway, in a white hamlet that doesn't even have a name—it's simply called the village—on the dilapidated windmill that stands guard over the handful of houses, there is a sign with an arrow: Hotel, 100 meters. It has two rooms, one is unoccupied. The proprietor of the hotel is an elderly man of few words. He is a former seaman and knows various languages, at least for communication, and on the island he is everything: mailman, pharmacist, and policeman. His right eye is a different color than his left, I don't think by nature, but as the result of a mysterious accident on one of his voyages, which he tried to explain to me with sparing words and with the unequivocal gesture of someone pointing to one eye and portraying something striking it. The room is very fine, truly we wouldn't have imagined it like this, neither of us. It is a large mansard overlooking the courtyard, with a ceiling that slopes down as far as a terrace resting on the stone portico around whose columns coil creepers with very green, robust, rather fleshy leaves laden with buds that open up at night to emit an intense perfume. I think those flowers keep the insects away, because I never saw any, unless this cleanness is the work of the fairly numerous geckos that populate the ceiling: they're fat too, and very likeable, because always motionless, at least apparently.

The gruff proprietor has an old serving woman who in the morning brings a substantial breakfast to my room consisting of ring-shaped bread rolls flavored with aniseed, honey, fresh cheese and a jug of tisane that tastes of mint. When I go down he is always bent over a table doing his accounts. Accounts of what, is anybody's guess. In his verbal sobriety he is nonetheless considerate. He always asks me: *como está su esposa*? Goodness knows why he chose to speak to me in Spanish, and the word "*esposa*," which he pronounces with due respect, and which is already a bit ridiculous in itself, would deserve a good laugh as a reply: Wife, what wife? God forbid!, and a hearty slap on the back. Instead I reply with the seriousness that the situation demands: she's well, thanks, this morning she woke very early, she's already down on the beach, she skipped breakfast. Poor lady, he replies still in Spanish, on an empty stomach by the sea, this cannot be! He claps his hands and the old woman comes. He talks to her in her language, and, quick as you like, she prepares the usual basket so that you won't go all morning on an empty stomach. And this was exactly what I brought you this morning too: a kind of bagel with aniseed, fresh cheese, and honey. I feel a bit like Little Red Riding Hood, but you are not the grandmother and luckily there is no big bad wolf. There is only a brownish nanny goat in the middle of the whiteness of the rocks, the blue in the background, and the path to take as far as the beach to stretch out on the towel beside yours.

I got you an open ticket, as the travel agencies put it in their technical jargon. Twice as expensive, I know, but they allow you to go back on any day you choose: and I'm not talking about the asthmatic little boat that shuttles every day from here to so-called civilization, but about the airplane on the nearest island, where there is a landing strip. And it's not a matter of throwing away money, you know that I'm careful with expenses, nor is it about showing you how generous I am, because maybe I'm not generous at all. It's because I understand that you have commitments: the things that one has to do, here and there, to and fro. In short: life. Yesterday you told me that you had to go back today, you really had to. Well, look, go back, that's what an open ticket is for. "No problemo," as they say nowadays. Besides, it's a good moment, because the tide is ebbing and it carries things out to sea.

I took your ticket, I went into the sea (this time with my pants on, to maintain the decorum due to a farewell) and I laid it on the surface of the water. A wave enveloped it, and it vanished from sight. Oh God, I thought for a moment with the trepidation that comes at departures (departures always cause a bit of anxiety, and you know that I am excessively prone to this), it'll end up on the rocks. But no. It surfaced and took the right direction, floating bravely on the current that refreshes the little bay, until it vanished from sight. I tried to wave the towel to say goodbye to you, but you were already too far away. Maybe you didn't even notice.

The River

My Dear,

I know you deal with the past: that's your job. But this is another matter, believe me. The past is easier to read: one turns around and, if possible, takes a look at it. And then, be that as it may, the past is always tangled up somewhere or other, maybe even in shreds. At times all you need is a sense of smell and taste buds, it's understood: we know this from certain novels, good ones too. Or a memory, whatever it may be: an object seen in childhood, a button rediscovered in a drawer, an old tram ticket, or maybe a person who, despite his being different, reminds you of another person. And suddenly you're there, on that very tram that used to rattle along between Porta Ticinese and Castello Sforzesco, then, as a matter of course, you go in through the street door of the nineteenth-century building; the main stairway has a wrought-iron banister with a serpent's head newel post, you go up two flights, the door opens without your having to ring the bell and you are not the least surprised at this, because above the rococo bureau in the entry, beyond the old Neoclassical grandfather clock, you see the antique mirror blotched with brownish patches and traversed by a scar that cleaves it from one corner to the other, and you recall the day when you said to me: A person with an illness like his cannot tempt fate like this, it's asking for a disaster. And at that point you understand that the door opened by itself simply because he, who wanted to tempt fate, got screwed like all of those who want to tempt fate. God only knows where he is buried, but the scarred mirror is still there, as is the day when you clearly understood what was going to happen.

Or you take a photograph album, any album belonging to anyone, someone like me, like you, like everyone else. And you realize that life is trapped in there, in the various segments enclosed by stupid paper rectangles that refuse to let it out of their narrow confines. And in the meantime life is welling up, impatient, it wants to escape that rectangle, because it knows that that little boy dressed in white with his first communion armband and his hands joined will cry in secret tomorrow (I say "tomorrow" here to mean just any day) because he will be ashamed of himself: some little smuttiness? Whether this is great or small is of no matter, because it implies remorse, and remorse is what we are talking about. But that ferocious photograph, stricter than a governess, does not allow the real truth to escape from its few square inches. Life is a prisoner of its portrayal: and only you remember the day after.

Look, it was like this, remember?—and in order to call this up I can't even quote a poem, not even of the poor-clothes-hanging-out-to-dry variety, always with its element of melancholy, telling of unknown and humble lives, so simple, with that simplicity only great poets can capture, or at least so they say. No: instead I can say there was a majestic landscape, of that beauty that's too beautiful when it's perfect, like a fresco by Simone Martini, in which a caparisoned horse leads an ineffable knight to an ineffable elsewhere. And I was driving my car. Slowly though, trying to follow the bends that furrow those hills and leaning my body over to one side or the other at each one, as you do on a bicycle, because I would have liked to be a little boy bowling along through that gentle landscape on the spanking new bicycle they just gave him at home for his birthday. It was a hamlet of no more than four houses in rough stone, not even whitewashed, with no one around. A hayloft gave on to the road. It was made of perforated bricks from which hung bits of straw that fluttered in the breeze, useless, abandoned in their turn. There are things like this, things that happen and you don't know why. There was no reason to stop in that deserted place, not even for a coffee, because there was absolutely nothing, apart from a lane where the paving ended in a dirt road at the corner of the hayloft, which led on toward the countryside: another nothingness, there in the background. And I took that road.

In hamlets of this type you will have noticed that there is always a little church or a chapel. It's because originally they were poor peasants' houses clustered around the manor house, and the peasants were devoted to the master and the Mass. And right there, at the end of the unpaved road, between two cypresses, exactly like nineteenth-century oleographs or postcards inscribed "The Heart of Civilization," there was a little church. It was abandoned too, like everything else. On the tip of the sloping roof, inside a brick-built double light open to the blue sky, hung two bells that looked like two cow bells, and those too unused for a long time, you could see. I parked the car right there, beneath one of the cypresses. Immediately after, rows of vines and cypresses painted the hills: the kind of place we like, in short.

All was as it should be. It was May. I took a leak against the cypress, even though I didn't need to, perhaps unconsciously attributing to that physiological act the reason for my having stopped in a place where I had no reason to stop. The little door of the church was closed. I walked around the building through the weeds that besieged the perimeter, taking care not to disturb the vipers, which love those abandoned places. In the gaps between the old stones grew clumps of capers, with flowing heads that for some strange reason made me think of Electra, and I tried to remember the verses I once knew, but my memory held no trace of them. I picked a couple of capers and chewed them, even though they were unripe, and I savored their sourness, almost as if that disagreeable flavor gave me back the sense of what happened, like some obligatory and necessary penance whose bitter taste reminds us of the sin we have committed. And I thought of life, which is surreptitious, and seldom reveals its motives on the surface, because its true course lies deep down, like a karstic river. I had told you: it's over now. But without telling you, because silence is karstic too. Did you think I had disappeared? In fact I *had*, by staying there, as if suspended in nothingness and wandering around a bit. Now I found myself in some place or other, different than the majestic one I was talking about before: a gorge in the mountains with sparse olive trees, and wild shrubs that bloom when the time comes. Every so often I would think of the shape of your crack, and I saw it as if it were a part of the landscape: the little clitoris hidden under the outer labia, and then the ample pubic hair, stretching like an arboretum as far as the first swell of the belly.

So in that meanwhile I was far away, and this is fundamental if you are to understand incomprehensible things, and the solitude was immense down among the mountains. I went into a taverna called Antartes, which means partisan in Greek, and that's how I felt too, like someone living on the run; I thought, you hide and fight, but against whom? Well, against things, you know how it is, things, I mean to say all things, for life gradually fills up and swells without your noticing it, but that swelling is excessive, like a cyst or like chaos, and at a certain point that mass of things—objects, memories, sounds, dreams, or daydreams—means nothing to you any longer, it's only an indistinct noise, a lump, a sob that goes neither up nor down, and strangulates. I was outside, beneath the vine pergola, and I was eating an exquisite dish made with lamb offal, looking at the steep gorges of Crete, those rugged mountains dappled with the color of oleanders amid the green of the olive groves, which is a dark, glossy green in that place, and I observed a flock of goats, which don't eat oleander, though they chew even brambles, and I thought: all right, I've made it.

A friend of mine maintains that, while suicide is a radical choice, at bottom, paradoxically, it is easier: one gesture and it's all over. Silence is far more difficult. It entails patience, perseverance, stubbornness; and above all it stands against the humdrum nature of our life, the days that remain to us, one after the other, so long in their small hours; it's like a vow made of crystal, a mere nothing can break it, and its enemy is time.

The way things happen. And what determines their course: a trifle. It was chance. I went into that taverna out of simple curiosity: to look. The room was bare, with some wicker chairs stacked up one on top of the other, and the tables placed in a corner. There were some photographs on the walls and I looked at them. In that village they worship two people: one is Venizelos, because he was born around there and there he had his headquarters during his battles; and you see him in youthful portraits and yellowed newspapers that depict in sepia his love for his people. The other is Kazantzakis, because he stopped in this village when one of his many sorrows was pursuing him, and here they welcomed him. He is a writer I never liked, perhaps because we resemble each other in our pride, save for the fact that in the micro-meanderings of our being the ways of pride are more infinite than those of the Lord, and in his case pride chose the path of courage and pride in having it. Mine is a completely different case, as you well know, in which pride can choose cowardice. Apart from his portrait, dressed as a respectable man (jacket, tie, well groomed mustache, hair oil, the profound gaze of one who looks at the camera as if looking into the eyes of Truth), there was also a photograph of his grave (well we can call it that), for his Church would not open its cemetery to a man it saw as a blasphemer, and his city, Heraklion, buried his remains in the city walls, and inscribed on the stone an expression of his that fits him perfectly, from head to toe: "I believe in nothing. I hope for nothing. I am free." You see the way things happen, and what determines their course: a statement like that is enough to demolish the plans of a person like me. Silence is truly fragile.

Forgive me if I change landscapes, but it is precisely because of those words that, on the day I was telling you about, I stopped the car in front of the church in an abandoned village in the countryside we know so well, and got out. And I went around the perimeter of that rustic parish church, almost as if I were looking there for something that might be able to stand against those proud words that terrify me. I know I am flying off at a tangent, and that all this has no logic, but, you know, certain things follow no logic, or at least no logic comprehensible to those like us who are always in search of logic: cause effect, cause effect, cause effect, solely to make sense of something that has no sense. This is why, as my friend would say, people who in one way or another chose silence in life actually did so because they sensed that speaking, and especially writing, are always ways of coming to terms with the lack of meaning in life.

So: now we are back on the outer perimeter of the little parish church abandoned amid scrub and stones. And maybe with a few snakes, for the poets would have it that way, although I never saw any. While the church was a humble one (ah, truly humble, it reminded me of the hump on the back of the tailor who made up my father's suits in my childhood), it did have an apse, with a narrow little door through which, I suppose, the priest used to enter to celebrate Sunday Mass for the peasants, arriving from his home opposite: not even a rectory, barely a cottage. And on that door rotten with woodworm there was a little typewritten label attached with scotch tape. A senseless label that said: "Choose Your Future Life Here. Admission free."

Of course I went in. What would you have done? You

who've concentrated on the past?—a hypocritical focus, apart from anything else, for someone who in reality is busy thinking about what tomorrow may bring, seeing that her past has left a certain bitterness. The future, the future! Such is our culture, based on what we could be—because the Gospels (and let this be said with all due respect) promise us the Kingdom of Heaven, a future tense at the end of the day—in other words, the future, seeing that the past is a disaster and the present is never enough for us. And nothing, you know, really nothing is enough, not even the gorse blooming in May for those who can see it but that I looked at without seeing, as we all do usually, until lapsing into that nostalgia for the irreversible, which for our kind is the absolute grave.

The memory of your cunt (forgive the insistence on crude anatomical detail) suddenly opened wide before me (if I may put it like that, blasphemously perhaps, I don't deny it, given that—abandoned or not—this was a holy place) and, unlike Kazantzakis, I understood that I was not free. On the contrary, I was a prisoner of myself. And above all I was no longer young, or at least not as young as when we met. But it seemed to me that I understood more, far more. Strange, certain associations of ideas: for example, that that crack of yours was not only a sort of vortex into which I would have liked to return, because for me it had been a place of indescribable pleasure (too easy), but more than that really a possible way back to the immemorial, to the origin of the world, as the cunning painter put it, back and ever farther back, until you come to the origin of origins, to unicellular nature, or better, to the bacterium, or better, to the amino acid, or better, to the Word, which must be the supreme metaphor of the amino acid. What an asshole, eh?

Sometimes certain associations of ideas come to mind that don't belong to our language, and you mustn't think this strange. Or words, because at times the world seems made of words that are the same among themselves, although the way we understand their substance may differ. The word *anthropos*, for example. This word that I'm thinking of, one that sounds the same to everyone, means a different thing for each of us. A word with such infinite meanings that not even the patient Linnaeus, my Dear, would have managed to classify them. In my case, a man alone, an extremely banal case verging on the ridiculous, given that newspapers and registry offices, city halls and authorities today call him a "single." But in my case *singularity* really coincides with the old solitude. The most absolute solitude, like that of the landscape all around, made of briar and gorse and cypresses on the hills. And that is why I knocked at the door and turned the handle. Usually, in cases like this, it ought to be opened by a lady of a certain age, preferably English, with gray hair and maybe wearing a sari, for she has lived in India, a person who has long meditated upon the philosophies of the East and who knows a thing or two about future lives.

And instead it was opened by a little old lady with a churlish air and a black kerchief on her head and down on her upper lip. With that opaque and apparently obtuse look of certain imbeciles who are nonetheless crafty in their own way, all she said to me was: Come in and take a seat, there's a chair waiting for you. That's exactly what she said: that there was a chair waiting for me. And so I went into a poky little room, which had once been a sacristy, with a little barred window, and a sort of little lectern and a single chair, the spitting image of Van Gogh's chair. I'm not kidding you, I even thought it had been copied from the painting, but it was so old and lopsided that they couldn't possibly have copied it, and Van Gogh certainly couldn't have wandered that far, his was the chair of a poor madman of Provence, in that café that served him as a boarding house, where the inhabitants of Arles used to play billiards, and those who missed the pocket ended up in the lunatic asylum walking round in circles with striped tunics the way he painted them. I sat down on it, as if forced to. Before me there was nothing except that sort of lectern that also served as a table. A completely incongruous telephone rang a couple of times, but the old woman didn't seem to think it was worth answering. From behind my back, from the barred window that overlooked the square full of weeds, there came a ray of sunlight that struck the opposite wall, on which there hung a map of the Universe. Does a map of the Universe exist? Of course not. But someone had tried to draw ours: it's expanding, they say, at least for the moment, then we'll see. Below the map of the Universe there was a hendecasyllable that I knew, *ma per seguir virtute e canoscenza*[1] and it seemed almost strange to me that it wasn't written in English: sometimes modernity plays nasty tricks on us. I thought of what my virtues might be. Looking myself over, none. And not even knowledge, despite all that I thought I had known. I was totally in the dark, at least as far as the past was concerned. It had gone just like that, like sand between my fingers, excuse the hackneyed metaphor, but truly I understood it in that moment: for the past, too, is made of moments, and every moment is like a tiny grain that flees, to hold on to it in and of itself would be easy; it's putting it together with the others that's impossible. In short: logic? None, my Dear. The idea of a future, even if assumed as a hypothesis, seemed even foggier to me. An enormous bank of fog, like those illustrations shown on the evening news when urbane individuals make meteorological TV prophecies.

[1]   Considerate la vostra semenza:
      fatti non foste a viver come bruti,
      ma per seguir virtute e canoscenza.

      Consider ye the seed from which ye sprang;
      Ye were not made to live like unto brutes,
      But for pursuit of virtue and of knowledge.

      Dante: Canto XXVI Inferno (Longfellow translation)

That was how I got caught up in the game. Not a quest for the deepest ego, for the one hidden in the abysses of our consciousness, as certain divers of our souls would have us believe. No, only a concentration on the most hidden memory, the one that made us happy in the past and on which we would like to model our future life, presuming that it will exist: just that point there, and that's all. I wished I had already met you when I first met you, and this, until now, was probably my most hidden desire. For at that point dream and desire coincide, being the same thing, at least for those who imagine even very vaguely a future life after the cells and the genome that holds them together have turned into dust.

The old woman replied: it depends. Sorry, I skipped a step, I had forgotten to tell you that the old woman dressed in black had huddled up in a corner like a bundle someone had forgotten, and to my question whether my future life depended on the desire I was thinking of, she had replied: it depends. Depends on what? I asked. She smiled like someone who knows a thing or two and gestured with her hand as if to say: Go, then you will understand. And she whispered: It all depends on how you will be thought of as you cross the threshold, son.

The situation was absurd, you will agree. The place, the flaking little room of an obsolete sacristy, and that kind of aged black-garbed secretary with the down on her upper lip looking at me impudently. And that made me irritated, but above all with myself, which always happens when you get yourself into an idiotic situation and you realize that it's idiotic, and you'd like to get out of it immediately, because you know that the more you persist in facing it and trying to master it the more idiotic it will become as you are steadily drawn into even greater idiocy with no way out. And I had understood this like a shot, but like an idiot I replied: bear with me, ma'am, but if I, in full possession of my mental faculties, were to decide to cross the threshold of that little door on which there is written "Future Life," I would think about whatever I damn well please, is that clear? The old woman smiled her crafty smile again. She touched her brow fleetingly with her index finger and said nothing. I mean to say, I tried to explain to the old woman with the calm that irritation sometimes fortunately manages to confer upon us, that in the precise moment when I cross the threshold with my right foot (I forgot to tell you that in the meantime I had browsed through a kind of instruction leaflet folded on the lectern, a crumpled bit of typewritten paper with the title: *Basic Technical Advice*) and I bring my left foot exactly alongside the right, as per those instructions, will I be free to think about what I like best, my good woman, or not? The old woman stretched out her arms, opened her hands on high and fluttered her fingers as if imitating the wind. Thought has wings son, she said with her ironic little smile: Thought has wings, you believe you think a thought, and suddenly, like the wind, it comes from where it pleases, and you believed you thought it, but it is thought that thinks you, and you are only thought of. Once more she gestured at me to go, if I had the courage. And this time it was a serious act of defiance, I understood that.

And it was out of defiance, believe me, that I refused to back down from that stupid challenge, in that stupid place, with that stupid old woman; and I certainly didn't believe one little bit of her sideshow tricks designed to screw a little money out of any passing suckers, like that gaudy basket (a round rustic basket lined in red, just imagine) where the price of metempsychosis was written with a felt-tip pen. Not that I didn't desire a future life for myself, in that precise moment of my life, but there is a big difference between that and accepting some stupid pantomime. Yet I placed the banknote required for metempsychosis inside the basket lined in red, grasped the handle of the door on which was written "Future

Life," closed my eyes as required by the instructions, crossed the threshold with my right foot and placed my left exactly beside the one that was already resting on the floor. And: Good evening, said the proprietrix of the Blue Dolphin, I've made *grenouilles à la provençale*, and the wine isn't half bad. It's a seven-year-old Bordeaux, the last bottle I had in the cellar, but a young wine cannot accompany a dish that took all afternoon to prepare. You let me choose the table, as you always did, and besides, the restaurant was practically deserted that evening: two old couples ahead of the season: perhaps English tourists. I chose a corner table next to the window dominated on the right by the open sea and on the left by the cliff with the lighthouse. She's been drinking tonight too, you whispered to me, a pity, she's still a beautiful woman, she's throwing herself away. Heaven knows the calamities she has lived through, I said to you, life isn't written on people's faces, or in the smiles with which they welcome you. The sea was truly furious. This sometimes happened in that little bay, without any apparently logical climatic reason; that evening there was no wind at all, for example. And the *grenouilles à la provençale* were sublime—as always. That evening, however, you too drank a bit more than usual. You said: this wine is impossible to resist. I agree with you. On the label there is a full-bottomed tower and the words written in large letters "Château Latour, domaine Pauillac, Bordeaux, 1975." You don't remember that label, naturally enough. But I do, it's before my eyes at every stage in the circle, as you will understand later. When we left, you were merry, and you asked me for a song about the sea. I chose Charles Trenet, although his is a calm sea, and you said to me: What a lovely song. And I set off slowly down toward the hostel where I had left a light burning.

And I continue to go down that road, inexorably, every time my life comes to that point. Like all the other points I continue to cross, those that come before and those that come after. That evening therefore, in other words this evening for me, after returning to the hostel, you say to me: I don't feel very well, I'm cold, and you wrap a woolen comforter around your shoulders and you fall asleep on the couch, while I sit smoking in front of the window thinking about my dead and listening to their voices borne by the sea. And then, the day after, I do what I did the day after, and you too, and the month after I do what I did the month after, and then after and after and after again. Until the day on which, without telling you so, I said that it was over. And there is an indistinct moment, I don't know whether long or short (but this doesn't matter much), which the adepts of metempsychosis call the anàstole in their code, in which everything starts over as the circle closes and reopens immediately. This is, I now know, a question of a tiny unbridgeable gap, because my itinerary lacks the segment of the little church where I stopped that day with the car, during the period of my anàstole. You know, that is a moment no longer accessible to those who have chosen to enter the circle, because it is that special moment (they call it the "void") when you don't know exactly who you are, where you are, or why you are there. It's like when a piece of music stops and all the instruments fall silent; that is the moment in which, they maintain, you come to terms with the lack of meaning in life, and so what's the point in repeating it? It would be senseless.

The only variants that are allowed me, as I re-enter the circle, are the different moments during re-entry to the circle itself: which can be the first day of our love affair, the second, the last, or any evening. It's always like that, ad infinitum. And it's always the same. For example, now I am in the fore-court of a rustic house, I have stopped beneath an almond tree, it is an evening toward the end of August, you are standing in the doorway because you know that I have arrived, and you come toward me with the calm of someone who has awaited a return for longer than can be borne, and in fact I am returning; from the village nearby comes the music of trumpets and accordions playing *Ciliegi rosa a primavera*. What's going on? I ask you. It's the village fete, you reply; you know, I spent Saint Lawrence's night looking at the shooting stars and I made a wish that you would return soon. Will you stay for dinner? And I stayed for dinner, and naturally, you made stuffed tomatoes and added some of the thyme that grows under the pergola of the house, next to the four o'clocks. And for you it's normal, because this was happening only in that moment, in that precise instant of time in which our bodies pass through that precise space that was the lawn in front of the rustic house where we heard the music of *Ciliegi rosa a primavera*, and you said to me: I spent Saint Lawrence's night looking at the shooting stars. Will you stay for dinner?

To make a wholly approximate calculation, at this moment of mine in which I find myself in this rustic Cretan taverna that I have reached in a flash to re-enter the circle from the beginning tomorrow, you must be almost an old woman now, as I too would be old if I had not crossed the fragile threshold I crossed. For life (yours, I mean) is logical, and it proceeds at the normal tempo. And probably you'll have an old secret lover, grandchildren, who also belong to the tempo of life, and your fair share of gray hairs, which for that matter can now be camouflaged with a simple sachet from the hairdresser's. And probably you will have attained the peace that the time you belong to provides for each of the stages of life granted to human beings. And surely, in the arduous process required at all ages of adjusting to ourselves, you will have understood at the age you have now reached that the nomadic life you used to invoke was not for you, and hence all that was merely a false dilemma. For, despite everything, peace always triumphs over disquietude. Which, in your case, is not entirely true, and I know this because I know your nature, which cannot contemplate a basket filled with balls of wool between your legs, or poetry readings, or grand-children who play the harpsichord: it was the other life that was true, the one we were unable to choose together. But, be that as it may, time goes by as it must: around the table, at dinner, the right people live with you the right time in the right place, because this is the correct measure of time, life and discourse.

I, contrariwise, am writing you from a broken time. All is smithereens, my Dear, the shards have flown all over the place and I can only put them together again in this vicious circle in which I continue to spin around to the point of nausea and idiocy, waiting for it to open at an unknown point—which will not be that of another life, but of this one. For I am not talking to you from the other side, but still from this one, although it certainly belongs to an orbit far from yours. If things were otherwise it would be too easy to get out of it: it would suffice to live the life that is granted us as if we lived in another dimension, a thing that sublime thinkers have some-times been able to resolve in no less sublime artistic ways. No, it's a very different problem. The fact is that the orbit is at once the same and another, I see yours and I enter it when I wish, without your being able to do the same with mine. I am here without your needing to be with me, or to know about it, because your orbit is unique and unrepeatable, and mine instead is synchronous with itself, and it spins around and around ad infinitum. And the twist, as I mentioned to you, lies precisely in this, that the moment of exit will occur only in my Present Time, in other words in that which I am about to be, but without being it: the dimensions have been reversed, what was only memory has become present, and what I really am or should be, my presumed now, has become virtual and I spot it from afar as though through a telescope held the wrong way round, waiting to re-enter it at the last moment, because that terminal instant in which we are permitted to run though our whole life backwards is an instant that I am condemned to live through unceasingly. And in that instant granted me I shall barely have the time to flounder in the air like a drowned man, and then: goodnight. You know, I think that in this escape from repeated time, which is a form of perverse entropy, there won't be even so much as a small explosion, as when in the universe a mass of compressed energy explodes to create a new star. Quite the opposite of the mad philosopher's idea that more chaos must be added to our spirit if a dancing star is to be born. What star! All you need is a tiny hole, and all this insensate energy will escape as if through a hole in a gas pipe and . . . fssss . . . fssss . . . all will finish in an instant, in the humblest of bubbles, a residue, a nothing made of nothing, like time farting. So I am sending you an impossible greeting, like one who waves vainly from one bank of the river to the other knowing that there are no banks, really, believe me, there are no banks, there is only the river, we didn't know before, but there is only the river, I'd like to shout to you: Watch out, there's only the river, you see! Yes, now I know, what idiots, we worried so much about the banks and instead there was only the river. But it's too late, what's the point in telling you all this?

Forbidden Games

Madame, my dear Friend,

The way things happen. And what determines their course: a trifle. It's something I read, and now I'm thinking about it. And then: are we the seekers or the sought? We ought to reflect upon this too. For example, a man wanders, of an evening, through streets and cafés, roaming aimlessly, as I do because I suffer from insomnia. At least I used to have Bobi; I would put on his leash and take him for a walk, it was an excuse. Now that he's dead, I don't even have that excuse anymore. I go here and there without logic, I hang out in the bistros until closing time, and then I get up and walk. The doctor told me: you are a classic case of *homo melancholicus*. But Dürer drew melancholy seated, I objected, for melancholy you need a chair. Yours is a different melancholy, he decreed, it is a mobile melancholy. And he prescribed motor exercise.

Yesterday for example I headed in the direction of Porte d'Orléans. To tell the truth, I didn't realize at the time, I was just walking. On boulevard Raspail the street lights highlighted the yellow of the leaves on the trees. It's early October. I thought of a line from a poem: the present yellow that the leaves live now. Present: that which is now and immediately is no longer so. That which passes. And so I thought about time and my passing through it. My legs bore me along rapidly, I was following a guided route, without realizing that it was guided. I realized this only after boulevard Général Leclerc, because between the brocanteur and the little Vietnamese restaurant, there was once a tailor's shop. And that's where I had a suit made for Christine's wedding. I was penniless, or very nearly, the tailor was an old Jew, the shop was on my route home, I knocked, he had cheap cloth, he made me a cheap suit. So, on passing by that shop that is now no longer there, I realized—without realizing—that I was heading for boulevard Jourdan and the Cité Universitaire. That's what I used to do, at that time, I would go home on foot, often in the small hours, because the subway closed fairly early and I would stay on to watch art movies in a little cinema in Saint-Germain: *L'âge d'or, Un chien andalou*. Stuff like that. I believed in the avant-garde. It was nice to think they were revolutionaries. Aesthetically, I mean. Along the boulevard Jourdan, not far from one of the entries to the Cité, there is a café that I frequented at that time. I used to go there with a group of Japanese students I had become friendly with, since for a certain period I had been obliged to take lodgings in the Maison du Japon, given that my country's Maison was being renovated. In the group there were a girl and a boy who aroused my sympathies. She was studying medicine and wanted to specialize in tropical diseases, but her dream was to become an opera singer and she took lessons from an old tenor who lived in the Marais. Puccini was her passion, and sometimes she would sing us arias from *Madame Butterfly*. We sat at a table, outside, it was winter, she sang *Un bel dì vedremo levarsi un fil di fumo*, and from her mouth there issued little clouds of steam. I said they were Puccini's musical ideograms. Her name was Atsuko. Our male friend wrote haiku and little poems, and when he felt like it he would read them to us. I recall one that went like this:

> Lightly swaying,
> the leaf falls in the October wind.
> Heavy is the time
> of a summer long past.

Sitting in that café we drank grapefruit juice and dreamed of possible worlds. In the mornings, in the lecture theatres of the

Sorbonne, an old philosophy professor whose name meant nothing to our abysmal ignorance would talk with poetic flights of fancy about Remorse and Nostalgia. We didn't know what it was all about, but it fascinated us like distant worlds that presumably lie on the other side of the ocean of life, on a remote shore where we will never land. But instead, here we are.

Yesterday my nocturnal steps led me to that little café of the old days. And I found it the same as it had been in the old days. The same youthful faces of my time, the students of the Cité who study together until three in the morning, when the café closes. Of course they dress a bit differently, and the music they listen to is different as well. Yet the faces are the same, and the eyes, and the looks. The jukebox into which we inserted coins to listen to Ornette Coleman, *Petite fleur*, *Une valse à mille temps*, is no longer there, but there is a tape recorder playing today's music: all very American. Next to the icebox the new owner has set up a small bookcase full of tapes left at the disposal of the students, who can select them and put them in the machine on the counter where a card says: *Libre Service*. On the lower shelf of the bookcase another card says: From the World—*Du Monde Entier*, and there you find music tapes from various countries that the students have brought from home or that were sent them by their friends and relatives. You can hear African ritual dance music, Indian ragas, string instruments from Anatolia, the wailing of geishas and all the diverse abstract methods that people have invented to express their feelings through sounds. On the last shelf, indicated by a card saying *Section Nostalgie*, there are the songs from our salad days, those most truly ours, the post-war ones, songs like *Le déserteur*, *Et c'est ainsi que les hommes vivent*: in short, the cellars of Saint Germain des Prés: women in black with red shoes, café existentialism, the musical anarchy of Boris Vian and Leo Ferré. I thought: Music before all other things. And I repeated the line out loud. And you came to mind, Madame, although I called you by your first name in those days. Certain words cannot be said with impunity, because words are things. By now I should know this, at my age and with all that has happened. But I said it. Without thinking of impunity. And you, Madame, you appeared on that balcony in Provence, do you remember? I am sure of this, you remember it as I do, but only from another point of view, because I was looking up at you from below and you were looking down at me from above. Do we want to embellish memories? Or to falsify them? This is what memory is for. Let's say it was June. Mild, as it should be in Provence. And maybe I was walking across a field of lavender, and on the edge of that field there was a rough stone house guarded by an almond tree. And beneath almond trees, sometimes, as Chinese wisdom teaches us, you can recall the memories of another. Am I confused perhaps? Then I am confused. But you know, Madame, that everything is confused. I am only trying to put all the confusion into a more or less plausible order. And plausibility presupposes falsity, involuntarily for all I know. So, I beg you to understand me. In the sense that in that moment you appeared at that balcony, *quand même*. You were naked, this you cannot not remember as I remember it, now, here, after all that after. Do you see? Of course you see. We had intercourse outside, among the lavender, beneath the almond tree. Did a tractor go by? Perhaps, but without its mechanical scythe. It was a long, serene, almost motionless embrace, and I cast my seed among the lavender. With a violet lavender blossom dampened with saliva you dried your most secret violet. Does this seem telluric to you or merely in bad taste? It doesn't matter: I didn't have only nightmares, but also heartening visions, and satisfactory ejaculations; lovely, really very lovely. Windows sometimes don't have shutters, they open onto horizons far broader than real ones. It's the window in my head. I don't want to throw away anything, and all this cannot be destroyed. Should I have stopped? Perhaps. Maybe. Who knows. But everything flows and nothing stands still, as the fellow said. And the sour poet made it worse, attributing the saying to a sinister rabbi: It's true, my son, you have fornicated, but that was in another country, and besides, the wench is dead.

And in that precise moment in which I was thinking all this, dear Friend, a wretched miracle occurred, one of those that life has in store for us so that we may sense something of what has been, what might be and what might have been. A suggestion that has to be seized like the posthumous prophecy of some ridiculous Sybil. There, a boy is getting up from his table. I look at him. He is short and stocky. And he is wearing hair oil. French features. He's certainly from the Auvergne, I think. And if he isn't, it's all the same. He heads for the bookcase with the tapes and puts one on. And Trenet's shrill voice, mawkish, maudlin, yet so moving, sings: *Que reste-t-il des nos amours, que reste-t-il de nos beaux jours, une photo, vieille photo de ma jeunesse.* And only then do I realize that on the table in front of me there is a blue folder bound with a white ribbon on which is written *Forbidden Games*, and I open it with slow, cautious movements as if in an ancient ceremony that has been waiting for me for years. And inside there was a photograph of a naked woman on a balcony. And that woman is not you, my dear Friend, but it is, for it is Isabel, but you too are Isabel, my dear Friend, as you know. It is an ineluctable thing. And on the back of that photo, tiny, neat handwriting, which I manage to decipher: a letter addressed to the very man who wrote it, and through him to me, and to you, a letter without a bottle that has sailed in goodness knows what diaphragm of the world to land there, on the table soiled with the rings left by glasses in that café on the outskirts of Paris. And I understood that I had to substitute for a thoracic surgeon and open up a chest, my own, yours, I don't know, and extract an essence that gives a meaning not to the aorta, to the blood vessels, or to the corpi cavernosi, but to a different biology, far from the cells, which drifts about in some elsewhere where life and writing, biography and literature must not meet, a sort of hyper-madeleine made not of words (too easy), not of megabytes, not of signs (for God's sake), but simple viva voce, which, as such, dies away as soon as it is said, just as the image dies the moment the shutter clicks.

No, my dear Friend, it's not the *senhal* of love-stricken Provençal poets, it's not the ineffable of anorexic philosophers, it's not the lightness that certain writers of this mephitic millennium that has just died would like to bequeath to posterity —if there will be posterity—writers who learned the lesson by wasting their talent and imagination writing for the benefit of manuals of narratology. None of all these things, *vous comprenez sans doute*. It's the clouds, dear Friend, in the modern sense, naturally. The clouds that cover more and more the face of the moon, which is getting farther and farther away, even though they stuck a flag into it like a toothpick in a cocktail olive. For the sky is getting lower and lower. So, *avec un ciel si gris qu'un canal c'est pendu*, another concept from the Nostalgia Section—but if the canals can hang themselves, the jerks can't, unfortunately they can't, they are laying siege to us. I beg you, do not interpret once more these ravings of mine as statements of poetics. If anything interpret them existentially. Even phe-no-men-o-lo-gic-al-ly. For the poet is rancorous, and the rest is clouds. Ferocity, the Obvious, the Politically Correct, Plastic, Cynicism. And if that were not enough, the Ologists, all possible and imaginable Ologists. And remorse and regrets, in any case kneeling on dried peas is no longer in fashion, a warm mea culpa with a spot of café crème, please. *C'est chiant, madame*, believe me. And then Science. Science, thanks to which the Fissionists cry out their eurekas: Hiroshima, my little mushroom! To the survivors, burns, irreversible genetic malformations, cancers of all kinds, my dear Friend. And many, many jerks. And tons of insensitive assholes. To sum up: Zyklon-B, radioactivity and barbed wire, as someone who knew about these things once said. And such things are hardly pesto sauce, don't you think? And in the meantime: lightness!, like a javelin thrower running barefoot on the lawns of Olympus. *Parbleu, quelle elegance.* Or: Life, the Life recommended by the Man-dressed-all-in-white at his window (have you noticed, Madame, what a lot of balconies and windows there are in this story?). Right, but whose life? And with what cunning ploys, moreover? And if we restricted ourselves to casting seed among the lavender, would that too not be a ploy, let's say a discourse on method? Take it as a double entendre, a metaphor of how someone like me can understand himself: the meaning of writing, for example. And so you, my dear Friend, who used to associate with elderly hacks, playing into their hands (or vice-versa), who knows if you won't learn how a story works, what narrative structures are, what you think literature is. Shall we be auto- or heterodiegetic? One really feels the need to resolve this knotty problem. In short, the nature of the novel, of which I leave you a small synopsis in this non-bottle, let's say a hypothetical novel, a little device of the do-it-yourself variety that you too can obtain by joining up the blank spaces between the dots, like the drawings in certain puzzle magazines that serve mainly for killing time.

I take a step back. In the meantime I had gone out into the cold air of Paris. The dawn (not leaden) brightened the gardens of the Cité Universitaire. I was astonished, or puzzled if you will, and I was holding this letter found in that non-bottle that I transcribe here for you:

Cela aurait été beau que tu gagnes la partie. Tu jouais dans la cour d'une maison pauvre, en été, tu te souviens?, ou non, plutôt à l'arrière-printemps, et ce vert, tout ce vert alentour, tu te souviens? La fontaine communale était en fonte, et elle était verte aussi, avec un robinet en cuivre, *Anciennes Fonderies* c'était encore inscrit avec les armoiries royales. Un broc, une femme nue sur le balcon, elle aurait voulu te parler, si elle avait pu, mais elle était une image de toujours, et le toujours a pas de voix. Tu passais par là, ignare comme tous les passants. Tu traversais quelque chose sans savoir quoi. Et ainsi tu t'en allais, petit a petit, vers un ailleurs. Il devait bien y avoir un ailleurs, pensais-tu. Mais était-ce vrai? Étranger, toi aussi, dans l'ailleurs. Les nuages, les nuages, qui changent sans cesse de forme, roulent dans le ciel. Et voyagent sans boussole. Étoile polaire, Croix du Sud. Allez, suivons les nuages. Engageons la partie avec les nuages, acceptons le défi, par exemple: comment se dispute ce jeu? Nimbus, cirrus, cumulus: ce sont les joueurs que présente l'équipe adverse. Voilà le premier qui arrive. Avec lui ce fut un âpre duel. Ah! Les moulinets que tu faisais avec ton sabre. Illustre cavalier qui participa à la joute, ton courage fut sans pareil et inégalable ta bravoure, magnifique ta générosité à défendre des nobles idéaux. Tu coupas les jambes du féroce nimbus qui lançait des tonnerres et des éclairs. Tu fis tourner comme une balle folle le cumulus rond qui adaptait à tout sa rotondité. Et le grand cirrus, tellement fier de sa 'cirrité' et dont la crème chantilly masquait le néant, il prit la fuite au loin. Noble chevalier, quel combat! Et tout cela sans armure. Puis tu t'en allas vers d'autres ailleurs, fragile mais fort, solide comme un roc et pourtant en équilibre précaire. Voyages par des sentiers qui bifurquent, chemins de Saint-Jacques-de-Compostelle, mers jamais naviguées auparavant, elle allait légère, ta pierre chancelante, chevalier sans tache et sans peur, avec toutes les peurs du monde et toutes les taches solaires.

Jusqu'au moment où le voyage d'aller devint celui du retour.

Cela aurait été beau que tu gagnes la partie, dit le tzigane aveugle. Mais moi, je ne chante pas le futur, sois tranquille, dans le journal de ce matin un acteur très connu dit qu'il est vieux et s'en vante, la patrie en tant que patrie même si elle est ingrate nous fascine et nous devons l'aimer (lettre non signée), si tu réponds à la question la plus difficile du Grand Concours et si tu maîtrises avec sûreté les événements en réussissant à devenir le point de référence de tout et de toi-même, tu gagnes vingt-huit points et un voyage à Zanzibar et, en outre, du moins pour cette semaine, l'influence positive d'Uranus te rend inhabituellement prudent, en t'évitant le péril de nourrir d'inutiles illusions. Si tu veux au contraire connaître les prédictions de ton horoscope, je te le vends pour deux sous, c'est un horoscope échu, tu peux le lire à l'envers jusqu'à l'époque où tu jouais dans la cour d'une maison pauvre.

C'était en été, tu te souviens? Sur le banc d'une gare, le balon oublié par un enfant flotte, et la femme nue au balcon a fermé la fenêtre.[2]

---

[2] It would have been nice if you had won the game. You were playing in the courtyard of a poor house, in the summer, do you remember? Or maybe not, perhaps it was toward the end of spring with that green, all that green around, do you remember? The town fountain was made of cast iron, it was green too, with a copper tap, *Anciennes Fonderies* was still written on it, with the royal coat of arms. A jug, a naked woman on the balcony, she would have liked to talk to you if she could have, but she was an image of forever, and forever has no voice. You passed by unaware, like all the passersby. You were crossing something without knowing what. And so you went away, little by little, toward an elsewhere. There had to be an elsewhere, you thought. But was it true? You were a stranger too, in the elsewhere. The clouds, the clouds that change form ceaselessly, whirling in the sky. And they travel without a compass. The North Star, the Southern Cross. Come on, let's follow the clouds. Let's play a game against the clouds, let's accept the challenge, for example: How do you play this game? Nimbus, cirrus, cumulus: these are the players fielded by the opposing team. And here comes the first one. With him it was a bitter duel. Oh, the moulinets you made with your saber. Illustrious knight who took part in the joust, your courage was peerless, and your skill unrivaled, your generosity magnificent in defending noble ideals. You cut off the legs of the ferocious nimbus that that was hurling thunder and lightning. You took the rounded cumulus that adapted its rotundity to all things and made it spin like a crazy ball. And the great cirrus so proud of its "cirrosity" whose whipped cream covered nothingness, took to flight, in the distance. Noble knight, what a battle! And all this without armor. Then you went off toward other elsewheres, fragile but strong, solid as a rock and yet in

My dear Friend, I'd like to make a date to meet you in another café, not the wrong one, where we waited for each other in vain. But I don't know where it is. And I fear that more than an ordinary café it may be a Café with a capital C, its eternal and unchanging image, a kind of Platonic idea of a Café where they don't serve coffee. It's true: no one can ever take away from us what we have lived, especially if we were looking for cracks. But, I wonder: what's the use in searching for them so much? Perhaps to find in them the Enjambments of the pensive versifier Tom Johnson, intrepid continuator of the Utah school of poetry? Saints preserve us! From one crack to another you end up receiving the well deserved pension of those who have served in public offices. And, when it comes to quotations, the time allowed, like life, has passed: the post-modernists belong to the last century. A propos of this, on the evening I was talking to you about, I too would have liked to put on a tape of a song that struck me as suitable for the occasion; the refrain goes like this: "But Gigolo and Gigolette still sing a song and dance along the Boulevard of Broken Dreams." But I didn't have it on me, and now the Boss wants to close the store, and the musicians are putting away their

unstable equilibrium. Journeys on paths that fork, paths like that of Saint James of Compostela, seas never before sailed, your wobbly stone went lightsome, knight without fear, blemish or spot, with all the fears of the world and all the sunspots too.

Until the moment in which the outward journey became the inward one.

It would have been nice if you had won the match, said the blind gypsy. But I, I do not sing the future, don't worry, in this morning's paper a famous actor says that he's old and proud of it, even though the motherland is ungrateful, it is still the motherland and it bewitches us and we must love it (unsigned letter), if you answer the most difficult question in the Great Competition and if you master events with confidence managing to become the benchmark for everyone and yourself, you win twenty-eight points and a trip to Zanzibar, and moreover, at least for this week, the positive influence of Uranus will make you unaccustomedly prudent, thus preventing the risk of vain illusions. But if you want to know what your horoscope has in store, I'll sell it for two cents, it's an out-of-date horoscope, you can read it backward until the time when you used to play in the courtyard of a poor house. It was summer, do you remember? On the bench of a train station a little boy's balloon bobbles forgotten, and the naked woman on the balcony has closed the window.

instruments. I'll sing it to you without accompaniment, the way I used to do.

Adieu my dear Friend, or maybe au revoir until another life that certainly won't be ours. For the games of being, as we know, are forbidden by that which, in having to be, has already been. It is the tiny yet insurmountable Forbidden Game imposed upon us by our Present Time.

The Circulation
of the Blood

My dearly beloved Hemoglobin,

A good imitation of the moon cannot be obtained without a complete blood-letting, in other words a definitive phlebotomy. This precept comes to us from the Ancients, who attributed the moon's paleness to a lack of blood. According to a Pre-Socratic fragment, only white lymph, that is to say cold matter, circulates in the moon. Hence, naturally, Proserpine the queen of the underworld, and all that follows regarding the life/death concept. And thus pallor and color, light and shade, sound and silence. For "silencieuse est la lune," and without a diphthong, the poet who said so knew this well, and that *i* of the missing diphthong is a long, melancholy note, almost a lament that brings a shiver in its wake.

What a privilege it is, my dearly beloved Hemoglobin, to speak with you of the moon. Not only because you are a chirurgeon who specializes in human blood, but because you are my blood doctor who made my heart race, that heart from whose beating springs this letter that I am sending to you, because you love me or loved me, because I love you or loved you, and with you I can talk of the circulation of the blood in a way that I can with no one else. And besides, as you are a hematotherapist, you also have a good knowledge of the white corpuscles, and therefore not only of the red that inflames our cheeks in moments of passion, but also of the pallor that is drawn on our brow when Our-Lady-The-Moon sends the icy beam of her melancholy sweeping across it. How can one not love the moon? Eternity is truly painted on her face, and as the ancient Persian teaches us, tomorrow is promised to no one. Let us drink therefore to the moonlight, O sweet moon, for the moon will shine on for a long time yet without finding us again.

You know, once I had to have a medical examination of my head. An over-industrious artery was pumping an excess of blood into my brain, an abundance that caused a feeling of illness, in fact devastating pain. As the doctor ran a kind of mouse up the nape of my neck, my neck and over my temples, he was studying a monitor in front of him, which I could just see too. And in that monitor I clearly saw what medicine could never know, I saw tides pulled by the moon, and waves in the stormy ocean of our head, and the cold North wind and the warm South wind, the sirocco inside the cranium, and I felt I could smell the briny odor of the winds ruffling my marine surface and causing salty migraines; the salt that in descending from the temples to the palate smacks of lost childhoods, of adolescences made up of tedium and useless loves, and of taking life as it comes, in other words senselessly, because taking life as it comes is always senseless—you've given up making sense of it. When will the cleansing rain finally come? Rain, when will you fall? And thunder, when will you clap? Oh, it's hard to say, my dearly beloved Hemoglobin. That's why the only remedy is to regulate one's own circulation. And how to orient oneself in the circulation of the blood, my dear, sweet, my most beloved Hemoglobin? Andrea Cesalpino, as you know better than I, discovered the direction of blood flow in the mid-sixteenth century. You know his *Quaestionum peripateticarum*: the veins always fill below and never above the point where the ligature is applied. Like life, therefore: always below events, always below itself. Cesalpino taught at the University of Pisa, the city beloved of that famous moonstruck poet who suffered from melancholy and tertian fevers and who slept between two mattresses to protect himself from the cold. And precisely in that city this fellow understood Cesalpino—

perhaps without ever reading him—he understood that the veins carry the blood back to the heart and not vice-versa, as Galen and the Ancients thought, and understanding this, there in that city, that lunatic's heart picked up again and once more began to beat the way it hadn't beaten for some time; Zephyr revived the stuffy air and he felt the illusions that he knew so well come back to life within him. But when illusions can no longer be revived, and the dawn is leaden, and beneath your window the nighttime traffic is on the point of turning into daytime traffic, and the street is glistening with rain, and yet the face of the moon remains framed in the window (not because it's about to set but perhaps because it has already risen), it really seems as if the time has come to find a scheme for interrupting the honest hydraulics that Cesalpino had discovered: time to make sure that the heart, which considers itself the principal pump of what is known as life, loses a bit of its arrogance. This is why it is necessary to make a careful study of the circulatory system— although this doesn't seem very important—to decorate the white majolica floor tiles with rose petals, one by one: drip, drop, but it would be more exact to say splish, splosh, for even sick fountains sometimes weep in red. Oh, but there's too much literature in all this, and in the world, and in life, I can't stand it! Let's stick to Science, which is a safe bet and doesn't err by a fraction of an inch; Science is exact, not like literature, which is so fuzzy, made of fuzziness. The fountain of science, for example, unlike that of words, obeys the inexorable laws of hydraulics. And if you turn on the tap (given that the circulatory system of that fountain flows from above to below and from the center outward, and that it's fitted with a relay pipe, and that the tap is lower than the tank), you can be sure that the water will issue forth. But, my dearly beloved Hemoglobin, at this point I wish to ask you a crucial question, which is the following: instead of opening other vessels for the passage of blood, why has nature completely prevented such a passage in the fetus? I realize that the question, put this way, seems quite beside the point. But I will try to explain myself better, beginning from the beginning, as they say. So: "In the fetus, as the lungs do not work, it's as if they didn't exist; nature, which makes use of two ventricles to circulate the blood, keeps the same arrangement both for those fetuses that have lungs but don't use them— because they don't breathe—and for the fetuses of lower animals without lungs. This demonstrates beyond all reasonable doubt that the contractions of the heart make the blood circulate from the vena cava to the aorta: the vessels are as wide and the passage is as easy as they would be in an adult male whose two ventricles communicated following the removal of the septum. In most animals, and in all animals at a certain age, these passageways are wide open and make the blood circulate through the ventricles. So now: why do we think that in some warm-blooded animals (man, for example) who have reached adulthood, this passage of blood does not take place through the ventricles? (As it does in the fetus through the necessary anastomoses, when the lungs devoid of any possible use cannot be supplied with blood?) How can it be preferable (and nature knows only what is preferable to all other options) that in adolescents nature stops this passage, whereas in the fetus and in all animals the communication is largely established? And, rather than opening other vessels for the passage of blood, why has nature completely prevented such a passage in the fetus?"

You must understand that I am putting this problem to you not only because at this moment I have assumed the fetal position, which seems more comfortable to me and, if I may say so, more protective, as well as being extremely well suited for returning to the earthly womb from which we emerged; it was no accident that in Minoan civilization people were buried like this: the knees tucked up against the chin with the arms holding folded legs, like a coil ready to spring into action as soon as eternity turns up—eternity being something that must be tackled with the necessary energy, because it's no small matter. I am telling you this especially because, before making my careful preparations, I went to the library to look for *De motu cordis*, written by William Harvey in 1628. The full title of the book is: *Exercitatio anatomica de motu cordis et sanguinis in animalibus*. You, my dearest Hemoglobin, will not find this surprising, but I was amazed to learn that we had to wait until 1628 before men knew the precise nature of the mechanism by which their cardiac muscle pumped that strange red fluid that circulates inside them, the indispensable nourishment of their lives.

You are an illustrious hematologist, my dearly beloved Hemoglobin (forgive me if I continue to use the name I chose when we were students), but I suspect that in your immaculate laboratory, under your infallible microscope, on the sterilized slides that lie at the right temperature in your aseptic glass cases, William Harvey has never been held in due esteem. And so I will introduce him to you myself, in this letter, which will reach you tomorrow, now that the color of a season ablaze in other days has probably taken on the color of the leaves of the creeper that surrounds the windows of your splendid office: the flames of autumn having passed over the crowns of the trees, the leaves are now yellow and fall thick and fast, oodles of them—oodle oodle, let's canoodle, we would whisper to each other hidden under blankets: half-light and mattress, and who gives a damn about sun and steel! And who was I? Why Johnny the partisan of course, the handsome partisan. (What are you looking at, my handsome partisan, what are you looking at, my handsome young man: I'm looking at your dau-aughter, high on the hills I will bear her awaaaay.) And off we go, on the double, but even partisans grow old, unless they die young like Johnny. Or like Marilyn. Just think, if Marilyn hadn't died so young and beautiful now she would be old and ugly and who'd pay any attention to her? Am I playing with words? Well yes, I'm playing with words. Do I like wordplay? Well yes, I like wordplay, especially punning. Pun away, my dear, pun away, at any rate here everything will run away, every word falls to the floor and bursts, makes a splash, becomes a strange circular star; what an odd perimeter this word splashed on the floor has, it looks like a fractal, because it fractures, it breaks, poor thing, it is a fraction of us that breaks as waves break on the beach, waves that are moreover only a very modest fraction of the vast sea. It is monotonous, above all it is monotonous, don't you agree? Just as this incessant dripping rain is monotonous, flip flap, now the drops sound like Donald Duck clapping. And what does a drop do?, what does a drop do? Cavat lapidem, that's what it does; this is why they invented the gutter, it's a matter of not getting wet, otherwise there's little else you can do but shake the rain off the way dogs do. Question: can life be shaken off too? For example, yesterday I saw Natalino, who ought to have been a man of glorious deeds, but who everyone used to call Talino. And he knew he was a Talino incapable of glorious deeds, that he was a blade of grass in the wind, a twig that trembled at the first breeze of life. Poor Talino!, we used to say. But you should see how he turned out: he is really unrecognizable. But first I have to tell you where I found him, in other words where I found myself. I was lying down beneath a tree, a huge tree. And I was at a small farm, probably somewhere in Spain or Portugal, although you can't talk about small farms in those parts. And so how should I put it, an "estate"? Let's put it like that, maybe you like the word better. Anyway it was a pretty place, so much so that I would define it as idyllic. Or better, Arcadian. For it was summer (and just so that this doesn't strike you as odd, yesterday was summer), or rather it was the end of the summer, because the bunches of grapes on those rambling vines were starting to ripen. And with those little bunches they make a light wine that's really something. Vino rosso?, verde?, verdicchio? Verdict. Well said, madame, verdict, the sentence is just, your honor. The jury of the people approve, endorse "estate," in fact, but you know what I propose? Just the country. Yes, I was in the "country," even though I can't say "my" country, because it's usually more correct like that, when there is a possessive adjective, and the so-called country suggests it was an estate. I was recubating like Tityrus, and I felt happy, for at the bottom of the meadow there ran a stream whose gurglings I could hear among the reeds. A little farther on there was a round farmyard made of fine rough stones worn smooth by the polishing action of the bare feet of peasants and corn-cob threshers. And alongside the farmyard stood a fine barn with a thatched roof, like the kind you see in Cantabria. And amid that rustic peace, as frogs croaked and crickets chirruped, which is what frogs and crickets must do, beneath that majestic oak my body was filled with an unusual peace, I barely had the time to say to myself: oh, how peaceful, when I opened and reopened my eyes and realized that that mighty tree was Natalino. Natalino! Natalino! I exclaimed, you've become a tree here! So you became a tree without telling a soul; not even Ovid would have imagined this, my dear Natalino, I'm glad to know you're a tree, and what a tree! Natalino gave me a smile of complicity, as he used to when we played cards together, when he would smile that smile that no one understood except me, because we always played as partners. But perhaps I should have realized that you would become an oak, I told him, I should have understood this at the time, it was no accident that you demanded an oak coffin, and what a fine figure you cut in it, that day when we accompanied you, while the band played the chorus from *Nabucco*. Someone tried to cover you with an umbrella because it had started to rain and I said to him, don't be silly, can't you see that Natalino is made of oak? And do you know what Natalino did at that point, my dear? An indescribable thing. He began to rustle all of his leaves; they quivered one by one like instruments playing an unknown music, and how right it seemed to me to look up to him when everyone had always looked down on him, and to see how he trembled with friendship and the pleasure of having me there, beneath his broad, protective shade. It is hard for me to describe to you the music of the concert that Natalino offered me with his leaves; it vaguely resembles one day when we went to that beach, in September, and there was no one there anymore, by then; all that was left was a light north-westerly wind rustling in the wickerwork of the hut where we ate and made love.

And then I opened my eyes, and I saw that I was here, and that maybe it was Saturday, a typical Saturday in the village, even though outside the city is bustling, an immense city, and tomorrow the hours will bring no anxiety or sadness, because I thought of the circulation of the blood, and how it pulses regularly inside us, patiently, for years and years, and how it is necessary to interrupt once and for all this respiration that unites us in a cosmic breath, to and fro, to and fro, with its eternal monotony punctuating senselessness. And I resolved to take the necessary measures against the metronome that marks the time of this eternal dance. Enough. For, as has been said, the man that we are was not made to live with a brain and its collateral organs: marrow, heart, lungs, gall bladder, genitals, and stomach; he was not made to live with the circulation of the blood.

I know that I am about to break a pact. We don't see each other anymore, but we agreed to write, and as far as writing goes, only in case of extreme necessity: a contract drawn up by you and countersigned by both of us. It's true that I am not in extreme need, because that extreme is already here, and you wouldn't get here in time. I have only an extreme need to write you this letter. I'll give you three guesses: One: because I don't want to depart in silence. Two: because I don't want to write to the woman I ought to write to. Three: because I dreamed of Natalino. Which do you choose?

Casta Diva

Eran rapiti i sensi[3], O my sweet lady,

And her hand, like a sickle moon, searched through your fur. So dexterous, her hand: accustomed to handling the jugular of stuck lambs—with gloved fingers as light as the wind, she sutures, salts or entrusts to God.

I am only casting parts, O my sweet lady, the inventor of this ridiculous theater appointed me director just this evening. In this threepenny opera, made of scraps, poor fancies, lucubration, nostalgia, rancor and yearnings, it's up to me to select the music, the scenery, the orchestra, the chorus, and the performers. Don't object, I beg you, as no one can object to anything, you can only resign yourself, you are Norma, the Norma I want. Oh please, come on, don't be like that, don't protest, I promise you that it will be one of those pastiches that you are so fond of. We'll rarely have the sun and the rest is rain that drenches us, it's a drenching rain, O my sweet lady, it's a rain that soaks you to the bone, and from the bones it penetrates the soul, like the damp gradually seeping, sowing mold on walls and gray hairs in men, but look, cheer up: it's not raining now. It's winter instead, and it's snowing, and around this mountain refuge the storm swirls. Can you see anything through the misty little window that looks out over the valley? I can't. The whirling snow creates a disquieting thick gray haze. Oh, yes, of course, you would love a clear, bright view, one without any margin for error, revealing in the snow all the footsteps you had to make in your life in order to arrive here. Tracks impossible to see, however, but in the

3 The senses were stolen away. The quotations in Italian translated here are taken from the libretto of *Norma* by Vincenzo Bellini.

end what does it matter, when it feels so good to be in the warmth? And in the warmth of a refuge that destiny offers us, while outdoors the blizzard swirls, what can you do? Perhaps you might like a bowl of piping hot broth? No, I won't let you have that, that's not on. These are three dreadful words, and our rudimentary melodrama hasn't yet come to its most dreadful parts, if there will be any. For now, let's try to keep up a semblance of elegance: in the warmth of the refuge that destiny has offered you, while the snow swirls outside, you drink a *cup of consommé*. You must say that, please. Behind you a motionless figure in the shadows, leaning against a table: the white vestment and the sinister air make him look suspiciously like a priest, the High Priest who controls the druid tribes with his magic powers—laudanum, needles, morphine. Yes, this is the man who makes sacrifices on the smooth stones of the dolmen, slitting the bellies of goats and scattering their entrails to the winds. He too, in the half light, raises his bowl of broth in a sort of enigmatic libation. But watch out! The moon is rising, let's hold our cups suspended in the air! Beyond that little window misted over by breath and the stink of armpits, the Pure Goddess turns her beauteous face, without cloud and without veil, to you all. The Priest, as I was saying, is as if frozen in mid gesture. Motionless in the dark (his face shadowed by a bluish beard that has fallen over his cheeks like a black wing), some drops of broth dribble from his thin lips onto his white vestment: I might even say that he is completely disgusting. Oh Norma, if I could, instead of "Dry your tears" I would have you sing: "Ah wipe off the consommé!" But that's too much even for an opera like this one. For the time being, wipe off nothing and drink your broth in the refuge besieged by the blizzard. At this point, having prepared this opera the way a weak case is prepared for trial, I have no desire to risk teaching the ants their ABCs: I prefer to entrust the show to a real director, a professional, inured to everything, someone who doesn't look in anyone's mouth for either broth or consommé. So now, I will step aside and withdraw behind the scenes.

* * *

"As you know, I have been appointed by the theater manager to direct this opera in which you are, my very dear Madam, the leading lady. Please don't hold it against me if I develop the plot as I see fit, creating an impromptu performance determined by the situation, by the siege of circumstances and by the viselike grip of the time. An impromptu performance, as you know, is based on intuition as a form of knowledge, on the rapidity of the understanding, on suppositions and on the short circuit. From you, Madam, I demand total obedience, the prompt execution of all my commands, an effort from the vocal chords—of which I know you have no lack—rapidity of bodily movement, and absolute immobility when immobility is necessary, all of which you can attain with the aid of your Oriental techniques. Can youth be conserved by clinging for the rest of our days to a bunk bed smelling of pine? This seductive theory is proposed by 'Stella Cometa,' an authoritative esoteric magazine according to which a scalpel plunging into the dead man must bring him back to life, but plunging blades into corpses is risky: the dead man is recalled by the metal, he awakes, he produces ear-splitting shrieks in the night. That, my very dear Madam, is the form your singing must take in this performance: like the blood-chilling scream of a dead man reawakened by the knife. You have all the vocal possibilities, and this is what I ask of you."

The man writing these words then took the baton lying on the music stand and made a light gesture in the air, as if calling up a distant music, directing a secret piano to play a nocturne. And as if by magic the flowing of a far-off keyboard was heard, and the lights were dimmed and a new backdrop began to descend, different from the filthy, steamed up window through which we glimpsed the Pure Goddess: a cloth of a pale blue color, but with a frame, a kind of enormous window giving on to the entire theater, thanks to which, as in certain paintings by Magritte, the exterior seemed to enter the interior and dissolve it. And in fact the interior disappeared in an instant, matter vanished like cigarette smoke into that blue leaving only the air, a large circular space, a horizon, a void that can accommodate any body, any situation, any action and movement executed by clusters of atoms and cells. With the tip of his baton the man transfixed a strip of moon and pulled it down into the center of that pale blue, an immense window that has by now sucked into itself all the other material bodies that had cluttered up the space. How strange was the orchestra conductor's baton that the man was moving in the air like a pen across a magic table visibly tracing its notes in space! The man moving that baton was not an orchestra conductor, perhaps he was an illusionist, a passing charlatan or someone who by some strange subterfuge managed to transform the notes into signs visible in the air, coloring them at his pleasure. He touched the Pure Goddess once more, and the large yellowish brass farthing of a newly risen moon became a livid blue, as it does to herald earthquakes, seaquakes, and other catastrophes for men. The moon's face was tender, like that of a mournful Proserpine who lives only in Hades, and its pallor lent a limey whiteness to the cheerful blue of the immense window; the moon prepared the surrounding emptiness for something lugubrious and unexpected, and how the music had changed in the meantime: the cry of an oboe heard in the distance gave way to the monotonous and obsessive lament of a cello playing fourths. It wailed, it wailed as the wind wails through the reeds, it wailed like the cicada, it sang a chorus that seemed to come from the belly of Proserpine, now become swollen as if she were pregnant. Whose were those sorrowful voices, full of suffering and fear, that gave you the shivers and murmured: Wild like wheat reaped with the sickle?

The baton made a sudden dart as if commanding an *andante con brio*. Two darts, two lashes, two slashes in the emptiness: and in place of the bunk bed that first occupied the scene it drew two vertical stones that supported a smooth horizontal stone: a dolmen. The voices of the chorus increased in intensity. The baton rapped speedily on the lower righthand corner of that landscape of nothingness, and the Priest, with his white tunic, emerged from the background. What was he seeking, in that desert? The baton showed this by moving rapidly to the slab of stone illuminated by the revived goddess and toward the entrails that had appeared on the dolmen. Without a doubt these were guts devoid of the human or animal envelope that had once housed them. A fragile, whitish tube of cartilage that ended in a big reddish bean, from which branched out other ducts laden with blood and lymphatic vessels. But these entrails led nowhere, because the body was absent. The Priest brandished a dagger whose blade glittered under a silvery ray. He stopped for a moment, raised one arm toward the sky and with the deep vocal chords of a powerful bass, he sang: "I'm bein' followed by a moonshadow, moonshadow, moonshadow. Leapin' and hoppin' on a moonshadow, moonshadow, moonshadow."

The baton flashed across the landscape and moved to the opposite corner. It wrote its music in the air and Norma appeared walking majestically with a veil on her head. In her hand she had a basket of prickly pears, and around her face, smeared with honey, friendly bees danced, singing: "Qual cor tradisti, qual cor perdesti, quest'ora orrenda ti manifesti, un Nume, un fato di te più forte ci volle uniti in vita e morte!"[4]

---

[4] This heart you have betrayed, this heart you have lost, this fatal hour will reveal it to you . . . A god, a fate stronger than you decreed our union in life and in death!

"Norma che avanzi a fare, Norma o icché tu fai,"[5] sang an isolated voice that had detached itself from the chorus. The baton moved to Norma's mouth, and obediently she sang: "Ring a ring o' roses, a pocketful of posies, atishoo, atishoo, we all fall down." She moved her arms like a marionette, jerkily, a marionette that obeys the strings that guide it; and then, taking greater impetus from her robust bosom, as if someone had pushed her, making her thrust out her chest, she sang: "Indian figs! Who'll buy my golden Indian figs? They're prickly but they're golden!"

Lashing the air, the baton moved toward the Priest. And he, who had remained gloomy in the darkness, opened his mouth (he had a little pink rosebud of a mouth, almost like a child's, which clashed with his bluish beard) and sang in a powerful bass voice: "Way cooooool, I want some!"

The baton moved like a beckoning hand. So come along then, it said mutely, the way orchestra conductors' batons do when they talk in silence, come, it's your turn, and have the pronuba step forward too, but let her stay in the shadows to officiate at the ritual. She is a fat, freckled hillbilly, with milky skin, and square glasses, she's just too sixties, and by now we are too far ahead in time, it would be terribly demodé amid this setting of human sacrifice and Celtic moons, but what Druid tribe are you from, so lusty despite your age?

So here's how the Priest came forward: silent, instruments in hand, he came up to the stone table of the dolmen and, oh, the miracles that lights can make, when the lighting designer is really on the ball! The navy blue of the backcloth that served as a window onto nothingness—were it illusion or reality, or a conjunction of horizons—that navy blue was transformed into a milky azure like that of the lamps in operating theaters, a dazzling light trained right on the stone of the

[5] Norma why are you moving forward, Norma oh what are you about?

dolmen. And on that stone slab, more like an operating table than some accursed count who wrote gruesome poems would have thought, there converged an alimentary tract, some surgical instruments, and some golden Indian figs. Figs that Norma, in the meanwhile, as the Priest was making the sacrifice, was scattering all about, dancing gracefully like the ethereal maidens of Pre-Raphaelite paintings, wearing a pale blue transparent tunic. And she sang: "Non mai l'altar tremendo di vittime mancò;"[6] and she sang it with the air of a pop song that goes: "Come fly with me . . . "

O my noble lady, here we ought to end this insane impromptu operetta that the director wanted to put on that evening. But, in reality, it continues. I know the ending: it escapes from the backstage of that ridiculous theatre, passes through the canvas backdrops and the poor sets painted to aid the spectators' illusions, crosses the show, the auditorium, space, time, and takes the direction that that Proserpine of Hades, disguised as the Pure Goddess, had promised. And what does it matter if the Priest was a barber surgeon or an engineer of seduction or a merry old man expert in scalene triangles: changing the order of the factors doesn't change the product. And you, in any case, were you.

And there they are, mounting a metal monster propped up against the back of the dolmen, a gleaming steel monster glittering in the moonlight. He, with his hands still reddened, grasps the handlebar and revs up the engine until it roars. She, seated behind, clasps his waist with one arm. And they're off! The roaring monster takes an esplanade and then a tunnel, where the dark of the night is even darker, and she trembles, and sings: "Sì, fino all'ore estreme compagna tua m'avrai,

6 The dreadful altar never lacked victims.

finché il mio core a battere io senta sul tuo cor"[7]. And she moves her breast closer to the centaur's back—he can really feel the beating of her corazón. And what a carnal frisson that flesh against flesh gives! And now the torso of the centaur has become a real centaur's back, shaggy as a wild animal whose hair seems more like the pelt of a wild boar. And she cries: faster! faster! accelerate, I beg you! And he accelerates, and away they go!, roaring through the night, as the tunnels follow one another with rare patches of open air, from which they catch fleeting glimpses of distant lights on the sea, and Proserpine's face is ever more smiling, ever more seductive.

As the speed increased, and the centaur began to feel the pelt of his back being caressed, he took one hand off the handlebars, holding the bike good and steady with the other, and his cunning fingers, like a crescent moon, sought for Norma's fleece and raked about in it. It was the diapason, that magic moment that they sought for so long. Yes, yes, yes, please, like that, don't stop, don't stop! The tunnel was coming to an end in that very moment and in the open sky Proserpine's face broke into a meretricious smile, and the steel monster took off from the ground and flew straight toward the subterranean sky, and for them, howling astride, that flying machine was by then a marriage bed, that immense bed as big as an arena where births and miscarriages, ancestral and conjugal menstruations took place, and the *libido rerum novarum*. A place made specially for them.

The only witness was a hair, left in the bidet.

---

7 Yes, right to the last hour you will have me as your companion . . . as long as I feel my heart beating on yours.

I Dropped by to See You,
But You Weren't Home

My dear, my dearest Dear,

Point of departure: once upon a time there was a wood. And in the middle of the wood there was a villa. And in front of the villa, a garden. And in the garden a boxwood maze in the Italian style, and two fine palm trees. And beneath the palms four wooden benches placed back to back, so that whoever sits under a tree on one bench cannot see the person sitting on the other. So, have you already understood? Sure you have, but I only say this to give you the point of departure. Because the other day you took me to that lovely place so that I might stay there in peace for a little, only for a very little while; until the next day, I remember you saying, or at most until the day after the next day, because you'll rest here, you'll see, your insomnia will go away, as well as this mania of yours for going from one place to the next; you can't go on like this my love, wandering from one place to the next, with this aimless mania for walking; certain friends of yours call you The Walker; you don't know it but they make fun of you, they call me but they already know that you're not there and they ask me in ironic tones: may I speak to the walker? If only you had agreed to talk with Sylvie's friend, what would it have cost you to go to Zurich? He was prepared to listen to you for whole afternoons at a time, and not out of professional interest but truly out of friendship; he understands people like you well, he's even written a book on cases like yours.

Dear, dearest Dear, I did this in order to give you a point of departure because yesterday, or perhaps the day before, I left from there, precisely from there, from one of those fine benches. I had breakfast, I can assure you and you can rest easy about that, even though I could have avoided it, because in the mornings I usually take just coffee. But the buffet was irresistible—you can take my word for it. Just to give you an idea: a table set under the veranda, covered by a hand-embroidered linen tablecloth with folk motifs over a brown background, really beautiful. At one end of the table, just for starters, a big bowl of yogurt. The yogurt is homemade, containing fresh berries picked the day before: strawberries, redcurrants, raspberries, and if you don't like them in yogurt you can also enjoy them on their own, because there is plain yogurt with berries on the side, and so you can eat them with a spoonful of sugar or some port wine, as you wish. The bowls are Murano glass, you can see that, and not the cheap kind either, period pieces I think. Things like that would cost you a fortune these days; it may even be that they cost less in Vienna, especially if you find them at my friend Hans's place (the colored filaments inside the glass are turquoise and form the most delicate waves), but my friend Hans's shop is always closed these days; maybe he's dead, and I'd be sorry if he were. Beside the bowl with the berries there is a basket of tiny brioches covered by a thickly woven cloth to keep them warm. It's hard to resist the temptation, I assure you. As for butters and jams I prefer to skip them. I say butters because there are three kinds, including a salted variety made by the country folk in the mountains who bring it in wicker panniers lined with laurel. It has a flavor that I cannot describe. The jams are the way they make them round here, thick, based on time-honored recipes, and, as well as the wild berry variety (obviously the specialty), there's my favorite, lemon, which is a halfway house between jam and candied fruit, with a sugar glaze that tastes vaguely of kirsch, but only very vaguely.

In short, I thoroughly enjoyed this breakfast, from beginning to end, rounding it off with orange juice and a strong coffee. Then a couple of pulls on my pipe on the bench I was telling you about and: we're off! If I'm not mistaken, our agreement was that you would come back to pick me up the next day or at most the day after next, which by my reckoning would make three days. Well, I have respected the agreement, and it seemed even twice as long to me. Until yesterday, when I said the old expression to myself: if the mountain won't go to Mohammed, then Mohammed must go to the mountain. I packed my bag, which as you know is very light, now more than ever, and I calmly took my leave. One is completely free to leave the villa, because the splendid wrought-iron gate is only locked in the evening. And so I began the trip, which I will describe to you here even though you know it well, because it is the same one we made together when you accompanied me here. Walking and walking, and walking and walking, as they say in fairy tales, because naturally I did it all on foot, and I must tell you, my dearest Dear, that the walk did me a lot of good, because for too many days I had taken no more than the briefest of strolls in that stupid garden. Perhaps you will ask me: but how did he manage to go all that way in only one day? Well, I just did. I could lie to you and cheat about the time, because the route is really long, and I mean really long, my dearest Dear, but I managed to do it in just twenty-four hours. And I'd challenge an old friend of yours, who claimed he walked more than me, to do it the way I did it, even though nowadays old Leporello couldn't do it, because he's pushing up daisies. But you must never rule anything out—sometimes a man gets up and walks, it's happened before.

In short after walking and walking, I chose as my first stopover a little town by the sea. Ugly, very ugly, in fact horendous (I write this with only one r because it doesn't deserve two). There, so that I might rest a bit, they gave me a little room with a fish net on the walls, decorated with two starfish. The inhabitants of that place probably think this picturesque, and the Germans and northern Europeans, too, who love the sea and go there in the summer. But the starfish must not have been completely dried—they stank like rotten fish. The only advantage was that this bad smell kept away the mosquitoes and so I had no problems with buzzing and itching, as happened to us that one evening (I hope you remember it) in that rather squalid little boarding house where we stayed. A factory-chimney boarding house, not in the sense that it had a factory chimney, but that grubby little town was full of them, and ugly too, into the bargain. But if you don't remember it doesn't matter, because that was another itinerary. Be that as it may, in the little room with the starfish I rested. And then I left again. The only serious problem is that during that ineffable stay I contracted a most bothersome irritation of the glans. Sorry about the somewhat inelegant details: it was a matter of tiny purple spots that suddenly appeared on the skin, causing burning and itching, even though I don't use my glans and it stays there hooded and nice and quiet, like a monk in a procession. But anyhow.

The second stopover was in an ordinary little apartment, which would have been cheap too, but with the money I had in my pocket, you know, I couldn't stay for more than a few hours. But at least I gave myself a relaxing footbath, it was an empty apartment, without a single piece of furniture, doesn't that strike you as odd? There was only a guitar propped up against the wall, and I played it for a few minutes, even though I can't play the guitar, but I do know the chords; and so I played some chords, because there was crying coming from the adjacent room and with a few chords perhaps the little one would fall asleep. I crooned: *come prima, più di prima, t'amerò, la mia vita, per la vita, ti darò.* And the crying stopped. The little one really needed a song, and more than that I couldn't do. Oh yes, I know that one should do much more for babies, but all I could give was a little song: do you think that wasn't enough? And then the time came to leave.

After walking and walking, you would expect me to say, given that you know me by now. But no, my dearest Dear. Didn't I tell you that that apartment was a bit odd? Well, I left the house, closing the door behind me, and I found myself in a kind of rocky, ashen desert, with bald hills that I wouldn't know how to describe to you; I could say hills like white elephants, but I fear that it wouldn't convey the idea, and anyway someone has already said it. And a noonday sun, implacable, I could have used a sombrero. I thought: in this inhospitable place I will collapse wretchedly to the ground, exhausted, and the vultures will pick my bones leaving them to lie bleaching stupidly in the sun, the sole witness to the fact that one day someone had passed by here. But fortune favors the bold: suddenly from behind me there came the voice of a little girl; she must have been tiny because I couldn't even see her in my rearview mirror, I mean to say in my glasses with the smoked lenses, which, when deliberately tilted, allow me to see behind me. So it was a little girl at ground level, or maybe it wasn't a little girl at all, only her voice, like the Cheshire Cat, and she was singing a little ditty to her goats. Perhaps she was an invisible shepherdess, or a wholly mental one, like those of the troubadours, who appear and disappear as the knight passes by, and this persuaded me to improvise a pastoral for her, probably a bit naïve, but what can I do? I was never good at poetry; I'm not bad at stories, but they don't rhyme, you know, in stories nothing rhymes with anything and there is no need for either rhyme or meter.

I'd like to talk to you about my stories, but maybe this isn't the right moment, you will understand why; I am writing to you in great haste from your house and I am aware that the architect wants to leave and the workers are giving me dirty looks. Stories. Or rather: my stories. What to say about them? Sometimes I think about them and I'd like to talk about them, but then the urge vanishes in a flash, and so I have never talked to you about them. But now I'd like to tell you, albeit briefly, not so much what they are, a rather difficult thing, but rather what they are not. As you know it's always easier to explain oneself in the negative, or at least I have always explained myself better that way, bear with me. They are stories without any logic, first of all. Between you and me, I'd really like to find the man who invented logic and give him a piece of my mind. And there are also stories without rhyme, especially without rhyme, where one thing doesn't fit in with another thing, one piece of the story doesn't connect with another piece of the story, and it all comes out like that, like life, which doesn't comply with rhyme, and each life has its own accent, different from the next person's accent. Possibly there are some internal rhymes, but who can guess those? When I set out the day before yesterday, or rather yesterday, from the villa, there was a guest with whom I had become on vaguely friendly terms during our chats together on a bench beneath the palm tree. Naturally we had our backs to each other, and this gave me a bit of a stiff neck. He is a young astrophysicist who came here to rest, because it's natural that the cosmos is tiring, just think how tiring it is to get up in the morning, never mind studying the universe. So I asked him for news about the universe, I say: What's new in this infinite universe you're so familiar with? And he goes: I hate to disappoint you, my dear Sir, but the universe is not infinite. At first, I confess to you, I felt almost indignant. Huh? I thought: What with all that we have read, and all that has been thought about infinity by poets and philosophers and theologians, and this overgrown youngster here, with the air of a baseball player sitting on a bench with his legs crossed and chewing gum, up and tells me that the universe is finite? I was about to reply: How dare you. But he went on placidly, you see, dear Sir, the universe began with a primordial explosion, let's say it was born like that, it is a mass of energy that is still expanding under the effect of the primordial explosion, and this energy is not infinite, but is contained within a perimeter, even though we are obviously dealing with a perimeter whose dimensions cannot be measured. Oh, yes, I objected, trying to conceal my irritation, but excuse me, my dear scientist, if this universe is finite, and it's expanding, that's to say advancing in various directions, where is it advancing? Forgive my curiosity. Toward nothingness, replied the young man in a casual tone. And in the meantime he was shifting the round pebbles of the driveway with his foot, he was wearing tennis shoes. My dearest Dear, you will understand my indignation and my puzzlement too: for us it has always been easier to understand the concept of the infinite than the finite, with reference to the universe but also to other things; try to imagine if one day you had said to me: I have a finite love for you, or if I had said that to you. Anyway, that this boy should talk to me about nothingness struck me as a bit much, frankly. Listen, my dear scientist, I asked him with a hint of irritation that I really couldn't hide: What would nothingness be, according to you? The young man looked at me condescendingly and replied wearily: nothingness is merely the absence of energy, my dear Sir, where there is no energy there is nothingness. And so saying he blew a bubble with his chewing gum and made it swell until it burst, almost as if it were a representation of the universe in expansion toward nothingness made for a dolt like me. How do you like that, my dearest Dear? But I was telling you about my pastoral in that curious desert, which really was curious, because a few steps later it ended in the sea. You'll think that it was a rather broad beach that I mistook for a desert, but no, because in those few paces the landscape changed radically, in the sense that I realized I had entered another scenario, as when the second act begins in the theater, and I saw cliffs overhanging the sea, and on the cliffs there stood a large, beautiful house, open to the winds and the spray of the waves; in short, custom-made for me, and moreover it seemed uninhabited, and so I stopped there. A grand night, I assure you, I'd define it as princely. On the ground floor, lounges, halls, a kitchen as big as that of a monastery with copper basins hanging from the walls and a spring of water that flowed from a kind of sink in the shape of a fish carved into the stone floor, and it poured into a kind of canal with marble banks that ran around the kitchen walls. It was the perfect place to fix myself a nice little dinner, after the journey I had made, and it was a tasty little dinner too, given that the larder was overflowing with delicacies. Just to give you an idea: as a starter a nice little seasoned prosciutto from the mountains, in its handsome paprika jacket, the kind you don't find any more, which I decided to slice open for the occasion, accompanying it with a piece of watermelon, which between you and me was really pastèque because it had exactly the same flavor as the one I ate one summer evening (now I don't recall when) in front of a kiosk on a street called Linden Avenue with my friend Daniel. You might object that all watermelons have the same flavor, if they are sweet and ripe, but no, that one had exactly the same flavor as the watermelon I ate with Daniel and that he called pastèque, beneath the wicker canopy of that ice cream parlor on the avenue, when he talked to me of Molière and his itinerant players; and therefore the watermelon I ate with the prosciutto was precisely the pastèque I ate that evening with Daniel, and if you don't mind I won't call it watermelon, but pastèque. Look, Daniel could confirm this for you, but unfortunately he died of a stroke, and it was you who called me, you can't have forgotten that. Then I opened a tin of foie gras that was almost asking for it, poor dusty tin of Alsatian foie gras abandoned in that kitchen open to the sea that had absolutely nothing to do with Alsace. To finish off, I had orange slices with a drop of sweet wine over them, then I went up to the second floor. The geometry of beautiful houses is simple: you orient yourself right away. I took the corridor that runs its entire length, I examined the various rooms and I chose the most spacious one, where there was a four-poster bed and a French window giving on to a terrace overlooking the sea and there, splish splash, you could hear the waves gently caressing the rocks. You guessed right: I slept on the terrace, it was impossible to resist that brick pavement still warm from the afternoon sun, and the cool breeze, as above my head the universe in expansion toward nothingness scintillated in an extraordinary manner. Good night Mr. Physicist.

The only snag was my itchy glans, sorry about the somewhat inelegant detail, which obliged me to wash several times during the night and to medicate it with some rather old talc that I found on the bathroom shelves. But luckily it was bearable and I got back to sleep immediately. In short, a fine night, full of stars and dreams, which if I think about it seems like eight nights, or eighty, like a lunar cycle, until the new equinox.

During the equinoxes a lot of strange things happen, the lunatics are right. I don't know how it happened, truly, even if I had to tell you I wouldn't know what to attribute the change to. It's like when a boat follows the current. The fact is that I heard someone weeping (praying?) and he must have been kneeling at the foot of his bed, with his head between his hands; he was invoking a name, you know like those invocations in the Brontë sisters' novels, and he must have been so unhappy, this someone, poor soul, that I felt responsible for his unhappiness. I don't know if it's ever happened to you, but you hear weeping near you and you get the urge to say: Omigod, it's my fault. And it seemed as if I heard: Leporello!, Leporello! Like a muffled sob that circulated in the air, polluting it. The moon has always had two faces: and then I recalled the competition for the job at the Post Office, to qualify you had to know by heart all the rivers of a certain region, even the streams, any region, maybe even an imaginary one like the metaphorical Ruritania in certain American musicals that many of our friends used to adore and that I found odious. Why odious? Because they were stupid movies, really really stupid, my dearest Dear, but one had to love them, and possibly wear boat shoes and eat avocados with shrimp as a hors d'oeuvre. Oh, what terrible times, don't you agree? It wasn't possible that some scourge would not come to clear the decks: a war, a massacre, a plague. Something had to happen, and in fact it happened, but you weren't expecting it.

And away again, walking and walking. The next morning I emerged from that night spent on the terrace, to continue my journey to your house and to see that woman still and motionless as a statue (it really has to be said), so motionless that I whisper *psst psst* and I look at her. And she turns around and looks at me, and so I get a good look at her, and she is really beautiful, or at least she seems so to me and I think that she likes me too, and she says to me: The doors of my house are open, the windows wide open, and love flows out of it with abundance and prodigality, with a kind of unwarranted confidence and abandon and forgetfulness. In truth, she wasn't supposed to tell me this, as I quote it to you verbatim, until after I left again, but this was the idea. It's only that you can't understand certain ideas clearly until afterward, when you are already on your way again. In any event I stopped, of this I am certain. The house was old, but very pretty. On two floors, painted in Pompeian red, the paintwork rather flaky, an external stairway and a pergola of wisteria. And a mimosa too, for women's day. The floors were in black and white lozenges, like the majolica work of the early twentieth century, which suited the aesthetics of a person like me, as well as my geometry, because I could stand sometimes on a black lozenge, sometimes on a white one, and play chess with myself until I made a checkmate. Naturally I was the pawn, the only piece on that chessboard, because she was the queen, and between us there were no knights. But there too someone was weeping. It seemed to be a little boy, or a boy who couldn't manage to grow up, and this is the cause of much distress for women and for all of us; a superfluous distress moreover, and it would be good to bear this in mind: children who don't manage to grow up usually become perfect adults. The only real problem is kids who are happy, as I was, kids who go off with age, and who take the opposite path, until the day when, pop, they burst like the bubble gum of the universe expanding toward nothingness. In short, the problem is that the schedule we must all follow is out of joint, my dearest Dear, don't you think? I mean to say: you stay there, you've grown up to the right point, and suddenly a child crying or an old man much older than you comes into your calendar. And this is what throws people's lives seriously out of kilter. The ideal would be for everyone, and I mean everyone, to be at the right age at the right time and in the right place, when we chance to meet in this little piece of the universe that is expanding toward nothingness, because this would simplify things very much indeed. But perhaps biologists would not agree with this eventuality, or demographers either, because according to them the human race would be finished off in two shakes. Agreed, maybe it would finish, but if we are heading toward nothingness in any case, then what difference does it make if we get there a bit sooner or a bit later? In measuring the whole business, the gentlemen like the one I was chatting to the day before yesterday on the bench in the villa use extremely abstruse units that are not days or hours or years or millennia or kilometers or leagues. I read this is a booklet he carried with him and gave me so that I might pick up a little knowledge: *The Amateur Astrophysicist's Little Handbook*. But to get to the point: I decided to leave that beautiful house with the windows open over the wisteria and doors wide open to love because I really needed a place where no one wept. Otherwise I wouldn't be here in your house now, where I have finally arrived.

So: I arrive, and the first thing I notice, on the path that leads to the garden but is a right of way open to everybody, is a yellow triangle with a figure of a man holding a shovel. I carry on despite this and, instead of the unsurfaced footpath flanked by clumps of lavender, I find a footpath paved with porphyry flagstones flanked by a white handrail all adorned with curlicues. Not only did this amaze me, but aesthetically speaking it left me dumbfounded, especially on thinking about certain publications you used to make fun of, like "The Most Elegant Homes on the Riviera" and that sort of thing. In any event, I proceeded. And in place of the terraced garden where until the day before yesterday we would sit watching the evening fall over the sea, there was a little lawn with grass of a rather flamboyant green. I don't understand how it managed to grow so fast, unless they laid it using pre-cultivated sod mats, which is what they do today, it seems. And on the grass, in the shape of footprints, small marble slabs on which you walk to gain the main entrance, in other words the veranda with the pergola of vines. A pergola that was no longer there, what's more. It had been uprooted, and its roots hung from the back of a little truck parked next to the entry. In place of the pergola there was a portico with red tiles, a really bright red, supported by two marble columns with two Ionian capitals. I looked up, in case you were on the terrace where you usually wait for me. The little wall in rough stone that surrounded the terrace where, safe from prying eyes, we would lie naked to take the sun, wasn't there anymore. In its place wrought-iron railings all curlicues like the one on the footpath. And the green shutters of the French windows had been replaced with a sliding glass door, of the kind you see in certain houses in American movies. I stopped, appalled, and I put my bag down on the ground. Under the little portico a man was sitting on a stool consulting enormous rolls of paper. He was very absorbed and paid no heed to me. Good evening, I said to him, is anyone in? I am, he replied, as you can see, I am. Oh, yes, said I, of course, you are, it's clear, but who are you, excuse me? What d'you mean who am I?, he replied, I am the architect, who else did you think I was? He looked at me with a hint of suspicion and I think I know why: my dusty jacket, my old felt hat, the jute traveling bag I have always used. Where have you come from?, he asked me, looking me up and down. From Villa Serena, I replied. He must have thought it was one of the villas on the nearby hills and he immediately changed his tone. Do you wish to see the house, perhaps?, he asked me kindly.

To see the house, what did he mean?, I thought to myself, to see a house I have always known and that I left the day before yesterday. In a moment, I replied as if playing for time, I'll take a stroll around the back. In reality I needed to take a leak, perhaps because of the anxiety that this unusual situation was causing me. I went down as far as the vegetable garden, but the vegetable garden was no longer there. No more bushes of sage and rosemary, no more runner beans climbing up the canes, no more tubs of basil and parsley. There were beds of pansies with rather limp petals, perhaps because of their recent transplanting, and a little boxwood hedge to make believe we were in an Italian-style garden. I pissed against those horrors and your friend Leporello came to mind, and why those red spots had appeared on my glans: because he had that eczema. I remember this because one evening a rather flighty girl arrived at his house and she was supposed to stay, but he found an excuse to send her away, and then as if to justify himself he opened his pants and said to me: I got this thing here out of the blue, has it ever happened to you, have you any idea what it might be? You see what leads you to understand things, sometimes a mere trifle, only because I was peeing on the pansies, and in that moment I understood everything, that's why I too had had that thing on me for the entire journey, for a very simple reason, allow me to tell you in French, parce que tu avais couché avec. But why didn't you ever tell me? You really are something, to say the least, you know better than I that I wouldn't have taken it badly, certain things in life can happen, perhaps out of distraction. Instead what I can't forgive you for is having uprooted the sage and the rosemary to plant these awful pansies.

I walked back toward the portico and that character goes: Well, do you want to see it or don't you? Sitting on some bricks there was a worker wearing a painter's cap and a shirt all spattered with plaster, and he too was looking me up and down. I don't need to see it, I answered him, I know it better than you. Oh yeah, he goes, and how come? I dined here the day before yesterday with the lady of the house, I told him. He gave himself a slap on the leg and exclaimed: Brilliant! And what did you eat? I described the dinner briefly, just to satisfy him. For your information, I pointed out, the lady is an excellent cook, she has a real passion for gastronomy. We ate a cream of pea soup with a knob of butter and a leaf of sage, chicken chasseur and a chocolate cake that the lady made with her own hands. A tasty little dinner, he commented, but if you had dinner the day before yesterday you will have already digested it by now. That's right, I replied, and that's why I'm hungry now, if you don't mind, but where is the lady? He exchanged what I thought was a knowing look with the plasterer. What do you think, Peter?, he asked the plasterer. No idea, the fellow replies throwing out his arms. I was really beginning to feel uneasy. Has she gone out? I asked, has she gone out perhaps? I'm afraid she has, replied this character who called himself an architect, I'm really afraid she's gone out. Has she been gone long? I asked. He said nothing. Has she been gone for a long time?, I persisted. That character spoke to the plasterer again. What do you think, Peter? The plasterer looked as if he were on the verge of bursting into laughter, but you could see from his grimace that he was making an effort to restrain himself, but in the end he let out an uproarious and rather vulgar guffaw. For a few years now, he mumbled amid his stupid laughter, at least since before the war, Sir! And off he went laughing again as if he had come out with a great witticism. I realized that I was getting really irritated and I tried to keep calm. Did she leave a note for me, perhaps? I asked. I don't think so, replied the architect. Do you think she'll be back very late? I asked. I'm afraid so, I'm really afraid so, said he, I don't know if it's worth waiting for her; in any case we have to go now, I'm sorry, we'll have to close the door now as we must be off. I'll wait for her to come back, I said, I have nothing to do this evening, maybe I'll sit here and write her a letter.

On the Difficulty
of Freeing Oneself from
Barbed Wire

Well: a sickness has wormed its way into these verses I'll
call it fence sickness, even though there's no need to fall
back on a term that goes beyond or comes from beyond
barbed wire.

(VITTORIO SERENI, *Algerian Diary*, 1944)

My dear Friend,

Sometimes one happens to spend the evening with friends and, by pure chance, the talk falls on one particular topic or another. The other evening, for example, I was invited to dinner by friends who live just behind the church of Saint-Germain, and in conversation someone mentioned a book called *Barbed Wire: A Political History* by Olivier Razac. I'll tell you right away that I don't know this author and I still haven't finished his book. But the idea of barbed wire touched me so deeply that I was led to make certain reflections, as if this letter that I am sending you were a psychoanalytic session and I were lying down on a couch. I don't like psychoanalyst's couches, because they are full of fleas from the patients who have lain down on them: fleas that bite, that sting, already sated with other people's blood. Everyone talks with his own blood, which apparently belongs to generic groups: according to the Red Cross, being in the O negative group means you are a universal donor, in other words your blood is the same as that of many others. But it's not true. Blood is too personal to be transmittable. It isn't only made of white and red cells, but is composed above all of memories. Not long ago I read in a trade magazine that some highly distinguished scientists tried to establish the place wherein lies the central and most intimate point of consciousness—which they called the "soul." They located it in a region of the brain. I don't agree with them: the soul is in the blood. Not in all the blood, naturally, but in a single corpuscle that is mixed with billions of other corpuscles and so it will never be possible to discover that little corpuscle that contains the soul, not even with a computer so perfect that it gets close to God (for this is what we are aiming at). In the history of humanity those who have understood and revealed the corpuscle that contains the soul are mystics and artists. An artist knows that in one of his thousand-page books, for example Proust's *Recherche* or Dante's *Divine Comedy*, there is a single word, one single red corpuscle, that bears his soul: and all the rest could be thrown away. Debussy knows that in his *Afternoon of a Faun* or in his *Sacred and Profane Dances* there is only a single note containing his soul. Leonardo da Vinci knows that in his *Madonna of the Rocks* or in the *Mona Lisa* there is but a single brush stroke that really contains his soul. He knows this, but without knowing where it may be found. And no critic and no exegete will ever be able to find it. Why?

Because there is barbed wire around that drop of blood.

There have been moments in which historical circumstances, the liberality of society, the apparent happiness of existence, have led us to believe that we knew this platelet, this ineffable and minuscule creature thanks to which life and knowledge of life were born on this Earth. Beyond any doubt these were the finest and happiest moments for the Cognoscenti (that's to say those whom Nature had granted the privilege of understanding on behalf of all the others). But the illusion is always ephemeral. When it does not evaporate due to its own nature, it dies from the effects of the barbed wire. There are two basic kinds of barbed wire whose action kills the understanding of our soul: the first of these is the one erected for us by others, the other is the one we build ourselves. I will not speak of the first: it's notorious, in this century of ours that Primo Levi summed up with this sinisterly chemical formula: Zyklon B, radioactivity and barbed wire. And in this epoch of Holocaust denial and revisionism—according to which the corpses in the mass graves in the concentration camps, and the mountains of shoes and spectacles still visible to this day in

Auschwitz, are no more than smoke emerging from the chimneys of the imagination of sectarian historians—talk of barbed wire would seem sarcastically tautological.

But no. Let's talk rather of the mental barbed wire that has led to the barbed wire I'm talking about: it's part of my spirit, and part of your spirit, O my dear Friend. I know this because I know it. And I know this because, having reached the year two thousand and the modest age I have attained, this barbed wire has pricked me, drawing the drop of blood that contains my entire soul, and yours—even though you don't want this. This barbed wire, contrary to what you think and imagine as a strait prison, may also be the maximum freedom granted us. For example: it is a window. This evening, here, at my friends' place, I open a window and I lean out. For some time I have wanted to see a summer storm again, and I wonder if it can repeat itself in the same way, complete with the same emotions that it aroused in me in an immemorial past. It was in Tuscany, it was already dark and I was in my car. I was driving along the road that from Montalcino goes down toward the Amiata. At a certain point, despite the darkness, I wanted to see the Abbey of Sant'Antimo again. It is without a doubt the most beautiful Romanesque church in the world, not only for the pure beauty of its construction, for its apse that resembles a slice of orange peel stuck on a child's ship, and for the tracery that mellows the pediment and the cornice of the entire building, but also because it stands in a valley that can be seen as soon you as you pass the first sharp bend, after which the road runs gently down, the way my grandmother used to caress my back to make me fall asleep when I was little. And alongside the sandstone edifice that turns yellowish when the sun shines, there are two cypresses in the shape of paintbrushes, and nothing else. After the second bend there is a large oak, an old, very old oak beneath which I stopped. There was no moon that night, but some black clouds that made for a low sky and stifling air. It was high summer, and it was hot, hot the way it gets in the Tuscany I learned to love when I came down from my North, so hot that the day seeks relief, water to slake the fire, so that it may be quenched even if only for a moment. From behind the church there came a livid lightning flash that lit up the apse like broad daylight, transforming it from angelic to diabolic. Then another flash appeared, at sunset, over the vineyards that slope down as far as the rectory. I was frightened by this harbinger of tempest, and I thought: better go back home. At that time I lived in a wild place that wasn't far off, in the hills. When I got there, the deluge had already begun, and the sky was ablaze, like a country fair at which the saints have flown into a rage. I went up to my room and I opened the window. It was a big window that overlooked a landscape composed of undergrowth and rocks beaten by the elements. The wild boar and rabbits who lived there were already in their lairs. In my room there was a woman who said to me: come and sleep. If she wasn't there, I imagined her, because when a storm breaks and its fury threatens you until your hands shake, you need to hear the voice of a woman who reassures you by saying: come to bed. I lit a cigarette and leaned against the parapet, and the glowing tip of my cigarette was a real trifle compared to the flames in the maddened sky. The electricity in the air was such that not only did it transport the thoughts, but also the voices running along the magnetic waves once studied by Marconi. And there was no need to dial numbers to get connected. Thus it was that I thought of my dead, and I spoke with them. The voices were clear, sharp, and they paid no heed whatsoever to the explosive thunderclaps. They told me about their life, which wasn't life, saying that they were serene, because they had nothing to account for in the life they had had. Then they took their leave of me, saying: Go to bed and make love.

And in the meantime, I was still standing there looking through a window giving on to the sky above Paris while on the stove an Italian dish was cooking all by itself. The evening was beautiful, and sporadic clouds scudded lightly across a sky verging on cobalt. Then the bells of Saint-Germain pealed out a festive carillon. And the summer storm of thirty years before returned as if by enchantment, I relived it because things can be relived even if only for an instant as fleeting and tiny as a drop of rain that patters on the window, dilating the universe of vision.

And from this window, I saw a great city, I saw the rooftops of Paris, I saw the lives of millions of people, I saw the world. And perhaps I heard the bells of the church of Saint-Germain. And I had the illusion that this vast horizon was the freedom that the barbed wire had forbidden me, or had forbidden my fathers. And I know that I can write about this freedom. And I know that, to you who are reading me, my dear Friend, it might seem the privilege of a true freedom won. But I hang on to my illusions, like you, because in order to find that tiny corpuscle traveling among the millions of corpuscles of my blood, the one in which my soul lies, and which could pass through the barbed wire, I would really have to pass through this window and have the courage to let this tiny drop of blood remain impressed like a painter's brushstroke on the sidewalk down below. That's where I would really be, and where you could really read me. But do you know, instead, who would have the task of reading me? The forensic squad who, with their instruments, would come to decipher my blood group. That's why, rather than all this, I am leaving you some words, and you must content yourself with that, because all the rest is words, words, words . . .

Good News from Home

My dear,

On this joyous day of family festivities, which we all long for throughout the year, I am writing you, my dear sweet life's companion, so that you'll know that even though it's not materially possible for you to be present, you are here with us even more than all the others present. So present are you that Rosa even set a place for you where you usually sit (it was her idea, to tell the truth); she used the embroidered linen tablecloth, the one we bought on that trip to Malaga, and she laid . . . guess what she used to lay the table? You've guessed it: she laid it with the very service that Uncle Enrico gave us as a wedding present and that, strange as it may seem, is still intact after all these years. Or rather, it was, but it isn't any more. Tommaso's boy, a little imp whom you have to watch every second because he's all over the place, broke one piece, though it's really a small matter; that tiny little bowl in the shape of rose petals whose purpose we never understood and that I used as an ashtray when we had guests to dinner. But since I've quit smoking I'm not sorry about it, and I hope that you won't be sorry either if Masino (I've taken to calling him that, the way we used to call our Tommaso when he was a boy) broke that stupid bowl whose purpose we never understood. Or are you sorry? No, because look, if you were sorry about it I could understand, in fact, I'd be the first to understand; besides, I'm well aware of the importance you attach to family things, for you they represent tradition, your forefathers, and even Uncle Enrico's little bowl can in some way symbolize the late lamented Uncle Enrico. But it's strange how you never attached any importance to the family jewels, apart from the diadem, which I made you wear. Take, for example, the jade earrings or your great aunt Fenèl's amethyst necklace; you always said that these jewels were too Moroccan, or too Egyptian, or too Turkish, in short, they smacked too much of the Orient, just as your great aunts smacked too much of the Orient, and so you always wound up leaving them in the jewel box, even if we had an important social engagement, under the pretext that amethysts didn't suit you. False. Look: our daughter-in-law, perhaps to please me, today asked my permission to wear that very amethyst necklace; what's more, her eyes are similar in color to yours, and it suited her divinely. Our daughter-in-law, by the way, is really on the ball, I don't think Tommaso could have found a better wife. Today she wanted to cook the main dish (something that rather irritated Rosa, but our daughter-in-law, who is intelligent and understood immediately, let her prepare the second course saying: Rosa, I'll spend only five minutes in your realm), a recipe unknown to me, and to you too, I think (I suspect that it's a nouvelle cuisine thing even though she swore it was a traditional dish from Campania), *tagliatelle alla Positano*. I know that the name will already be irritating you, because you will be imagining a bunch of petty snobs like those we used to meet certain summers, the grapefruit for breakfast kind, breakfast being at midday, and then back to the beach again to sleep. But that's not it at all. The sauce is made with one egg per person (we didn't count Masino), yolk and white beaten together, and then mixed with grated parmesan, slices of zucchini barely dipped in oil, a pinch of pepper and a knob of butter. Apparently the secret is to avoid cooking the egg when you pour the mix over the boiling hot tagliatelle, and then you have to get busy with the ladle, and it's better if two people do the stirring. It was a splendid day, just the way an Easter Monday should be. The first item on the TV news, naturally, featured those vacationers who, having taken advantage of this April long weekend (as you know Tuesday is a holiday too), departed en masse toward places of *"villeggiatura,"* as they will call holiday resorts on television; they don't know that the word *villeggiatura* comes from villas, in which people once used to spend their vacations, but these poor wretches stuck in traffic miles and miles long on the freeways in order to enjoy an extra day away from home don't strike me as vacationers so much as convicts on a chain gang. But the high point of the news was when the anchorwoman, a flashy blonde with a shrill voice and a breathtaking décolletage and provocative crimson lips, with the look of a woman who was shooting a scene for a risqué movie, announced to viewers: following a smash involving eight cars on such and such a freeway, three cars caught fire and the passengers, seven persons in all, including a little boy, were burnt to death; for the present it is impossible to identify the victims, largely because the license plates melted in the heat of the blaze. The police are working to find the next of kin through the chassis registration numbers, but these are hard to extricate from the tangle of wreckage. And now, she added, our news program continues with some spectacular footage from the qualifying stages of a grand prix auto racing event held yesterday in the United States, another terrifying smash, as you can see, but fortunately one without any victims; the driver emerged unscathed from the vehicle and even made the victory sign with his fingers.

This is how things go around here, my dear, so much so that I often envy the place where you find yourself. We are living in truly strange times. Still today, on television, I saw a program about some African country, I don't know which, afflicted by a scourge, or several scourges: you could see skeletal children with enormous bellies and wizened little faces all enormous eyes, and everyone covered with flies. And a little later, but on a different program, where elegantly dressed politicians are invited to talk, a guest said that one of the foremost planks in his party's platform was the problem of adoption: because we have to make things easier, he explained with a smile, the bureaucratic red tape surrounding adoption in our country is too complex, many parents desirous of a child are waiting impatiently to adopt. In short: every year in the world some millions of children die of disease and malnutrition, but take consolation, dear viewers, for if my party wins the elections next year I'll have you adopt a hundred or so more.

In the afternoon I had a nap on the couch, the usual one, you know that a quarter hour is all I need, then I played chess with Tommaso. I don't know if I've already told you that Tommaso doesn't tell lies anymore, which was always a worry for you, and he confides in me. I had sensed that there was something wrong: sometimes his gaze is absent, other times he is cheerful for no reason, other times again he replies as if he has gotten hold of the wrong end of the stick. I took advantage of our being alone together and I asked him the question point blank. Tommaso, I say, there's another woman, isn't there? And he goes: Yes. What d'you mean yes, I say, what d'you mean yes? You asked me and I answered you, he concluded. Tommaso has always felt a kind of special attraction for women, since he was little more than a child, as you know better than I. But with that wife of his—beautiful, good, a first class companion, and what a mother, if you could only see how she's bringing up Masino—Tommaso, I tell him, with a wife like yours, how can you? He looks at me and tears come into his eyes. It's a passing fancy, he murmured, you'll see that it's a passing fancy, perhaps it's a little fixation, maybe I'm a bit like mom, I'll get over it soon, you'll see. I felt a bit sorry for him. He's going a touch gray at the temples, he's gone gray faster than I, my hair stayed black until I was over fifty. I told him: Tommaso, confide in me. And, throwing out his arms, he replied: Drop it dad, you know what life's like, you never know which direction it's taking, but it'll resume its normal course, you'll see. It will strike you as odd but that reassured me. It's curious that a father feels reassured by a son when he worries precisely because things are going wrong for the son. You see, as far as I'm concerned, these days I take things as they come. I have withdrawn into private life, as they say. My colleague Caponi, the fellow who won the contract for the development scheme for our town and who struck you at the time as a shark, is only a little fish in reality, the poor thing. He's bought himself a plot of land near our house, a building plot, and he's built himself a house in which to spend his retirement. The design is his, obviously, and this will strike you as strange too, but the house is not that ugly. Not that he's much of an architect, he never was, I was better, even on the faculty everyone knew this, but at least the house came out all right for him. There is a big picture window overlooking a sloping garden (it has an eastern exposure) and from there it dominates the entire valley. As a spatial concept it closely resembles (too closely, I'd say) Wright's prairie house over the waterfall, in a modest way obviously, especially because there's no waterfall, yet as a whole it has a pleasing look, and the interior is tastefully decorated. Last week he invited me to dinner, and I spent a decent evening there. He called me: My dear friend, says he, we haven't seen each other in ages, now that we are neighbors it seems silly for both of us to feign indifference, and besides I'd really love to see you, my wife and I are here alone, you know, my son has moved to Paris permanently since he got married; would you come to dinner with us tomorrow evening?

We talked about the old days on the faculty, and about Tom, Dick and Harry. And about certain episodes, for example a department meeting that I had completely erased from my memory but that he remembered down to the smallest detail, when Sabatini (do you remember the fellow who taught aesthetics, who looked like a Saint Bernard but was nice as pie) nearly beat up the administrative director because of a research grant about which the latter had made some rather heavy-handed allusions. And inevitably the conversation got around to you, even though I tried to say as little as possible: yes, of course, I was fine, Tommaso and his wife are very considerate, they call me every evening, do I have a fantastic daughter-in-law? Yes I have a fantastic daughter-in-law, in any case Tommaso deserved a person like that, Tommaso was a good sort. Was it true that he had become a magnate of high finance? Well now, let's not exaggerate, even at school Tommaso had always been an ace at math, he was unbeatable when it came to numbers and figures, it's a natural gift, after graduating in economics he served his apprenticeship in a big Milanese bank, but the credit always goes to the teacher, even though you need a pupil who learns, and Tommaso had learned really well, the credit however was due above all to that financial genius who had taken a shine to him and who had taught him everything, but to go from that to calling Tommaso a magnate of high finance was stretching it a bit, let's say someone who counts in the world of finance. Yes it was true that he was an adviser to the minister, but only sporadically, when he was called upon to give advice, it wasn't his profession, especially because someone like him cannot spend his days cooped up in a ministry, you'll both understand, Tommaso needs to spend time in London or New York at least once a month, he goes there, sounds out the Stock Exchange, it doesn't take him very long, you know, Tommaso's like that, he stays in Wall Street for three days and he has already sensed which way the wind is going to blow in Europe over the next three months, he's a real wizard at these things. And then Caponi's wife goes: Sure, who would have ever imagined it, your Tommaso having been such a difficult boy, with such a tormented adolescence. Difficult up to a certain point, I toned it down, keeping things as vague as possible: You know, Mrs. Caponi, when they are kids, kids can seem difficult, but then it's a passing phase. Unfortunately they don't realize what harm they can cause, Mrs. Caponi went on, and maybe they get over the phase when irreparable damage has already been done. I tried to change the subject, and with a bit of effort I managed, even though Caponi's wife was determined to get out of me what had happened; she must have thought: Finally we're going to understand something about this whole business, tonight is *the* night. But it wasn't, my dear, I assure you, you know how I have always been anxious to keep my mouth shut about what happened with Tommaso. Moreover I must tell you—I really must tell you this, forgive me—that Tommaso has always done everything possible to prove you right. He acted unconsciously, that's clear, by now in fact it's more than clear, given what he has become, with his self-confidence and all. But at first he behaved in such a way that no one could contradict or gainsay you, trying in every way to emphasize his so-called "problems," the problems that he caused you, I mean to say. In short, a sort of "compulsive guilt." And, mind you, that's not just the definition proposed by Greta, who was the first to treat him for you and who did so with a great deal of care and patience, but also by an eminent clinician, a psychiatrist to whom I took Tommaso in Geneva six months after the event. The idea to try this was Greta's, because even she couldn't make head or tail of things anymore; after your departure I was the one who had to take him to his sessions, and one fine day Greta said to me: There's something I don't get about this whole business, and I'm not going to find out what it is on my own, maybe because as a therapist I'm not up to such a complicated case. We need some extra help here, and I know a leading light in child psychology whose opinion I'd like to hear. And she sent me to the professor in Geneva giving me all the notes she had taken during the sessions of that year when you were bringing Tommaso to her, including those times when you had to tell the story because Tommaso had stayed at home. On that day too, in Geneva, Tommaso did all he could to prove you right. The train journey was hell. He was restless, he was bothering the woman who was sitting in our compartment, he went out into the corridor and tripped a pretty girl who was passing, and she very nearly slapped him. But at the psychiatrist's he sat there good as gold, angelic, looking at the ceiling. The professor was a robust man, with solid wrists, blue eyes and reddish hair, he looked more like a workman than a great psychiatrist, and he made himself clear when he spoke: in short, a person who inspired you with confidence. I would prefer it if you left us alone, he said to me, and he had me take a seat in the little waiting room next door, and then he told Tommaso to undress and to lie down on the couch. It was a very long examination, about an hour. Then he called me back in and Tommasino was sitting on a stool, dressed once more, with his eyes on the ceiling. This time it was his turn to go out, and the professor had him take the seat in the waiting room I had occupied before. He looked at me, shook his head and set to examining the papers Greta had sent him. He was reading and murmuring: This woman is mad. At a certain point he asks me: How old is your son? Twelve, almost thirteen, I replied. He made no comment and carried on reading, muttering: this complex . . . that complex . . . here's another complex . . . manias . . . non-identifiable disturbances . . . How old did you say your son was?, he asked me again. Twelve, almost thirteen, I repeated. He gave me back the papers and looked me straight in the eye. My dear sir, he said, as far as regards the genital sphere, and I'm referring to the male organ, your son could be twenty, or thirty; look, sir, he is exactly like you or me, and maybe even a little more, I don't know if I'm making myself clear. No, I said, you're not making yourself all that clear. Who is this madwoman?, he persisted. I didn't reply, because I didn't like to put Greta in that situation, what's more it was she who had sent me to him. Did you reach puberty so precociously?, he asked me. No, I replied, I was normal. Oh well, said he, norms are like statistics, and in your family? To the best of my knowledge, no, I said. There is a science called endocrinology, said the professor, it is the study of the hormonal system; look, that's all there is to it, your son has a hormonal system that is a bit outside the norm for his age, and the same holds for the related organs. Obviously, he doesn't know what to do with them, his hormonal system prompts him to use them for the purpose nature created them for, but tell me, would you have known what to do with them at twelve?; of course not, so, just have a little patience, let him grow up a bit, content yourself with waiting five or six years, and everything will return to the synchrony that his hormonal system has at present thrown slightly out of phase. Now have I made myself clear? Perfectly, I replied. He slapped his hand down on the papers in front of him and asked me once more: who is this madwoman? As you can understand, the situation was really embarrassing: if I had found that professor who had finally managed to solve the problem that had tormented us so much then I owed this to Greta, who as well as being a highly respectable therapist has always been your best friend. So I replied: she is a colleague of yours, professor, a therapist we have faith in, but I would prefer not to give her name. I'm not referring to her, continued the professor, I'm referring to the delirium of this other person; hers is a real delirium, she sees specters everywhere, she doesn't even understand that she is so ill, and that's what's worrying, this is really a person in a tragic situation. She was, I replied, she committed suicide six months ago. She was . . . ? he asked. Tommaso's mother, I said, my wife. Mothers are hasty at times, said the doctor, and they worry too much about their children.

My dear, it would be superfluous to tell you of the grief we all felt when you threw yourself down the well and, as I told you, Tommaso, who without understanding had understood, played at being abnormal for another four or five years rather than renege on you. Then he stopped, in fact he became normal, very normal indeed, even too much so. I like to see him so normal, but I assure you that spending a whole day with him is a deadly bore, I don't know how his wife can stand him, she's a woman full of curiosity and imagination; she is the one who should find a lover, and not the other way around as is the case. But I wouldn't like you to think that Greta and I lived together straight off. Sure, the opinion given by the professor in Geneva contributed to a rapport, a reciprocal understanding. Besides, we have never lived together in the real sense of the term, I mean living in the same house. I tried it for a few months, but I just couldn't handle it, and I preferred to go back to our old house, where at least there was your dear presence. The thing is that Greta, poor thing, with all her virtues, is in her turn the most boring person in the world, maybe because she is the most normal woman in the world: never an impulse, never a slightly crazy idea, never an intuition, never a sudden whim or a caprice like the ones you used to have—the things that give life flavor. On coming back home in the evening, tired after all her patients' tales, she would eat a salad and a piece of fruit and take a seat in front of the television: at a certain point she would even prepare herself a tray in order to have a better view of the television and she would dine there; she was fascinated by an unctuous journalist who interviewed all the politicians in the country, unbelievable, and I would go off to bed to read. You know, at a certain point I realized that true madness is normality, don't you agree?

Sure, it's a real pity that you did what you did. By now the years have passed, lots of them, my dear, really lots. Yet see how we remember you still, how I remember you. You're always with me, you know, you accompany me in every moment of my life. Even though my life functions at only ten per cent these days. But when it used to function at a hundred per cent like yours, how beautiful it was, and how great was our passion. So great that the cells of my body are still steeped in it, like a sponge that has conserved the seawater that nourished it. For afterward, my dear, it was only sweet water, often cloying, and what sense is there, I wonder, in living on with no salt to refresh my palate?

What's the Use of a Harp
with Only One String?

Si 'sta voce te sceta 'int'a nuttata
Mentre t'astrigne 'o sposo tuio vicino,
statte scetata, si vuò stà scetata,
ma fa' vedè ca duorme, a suonno chino*

(*Voce 'e notte*, a Neapolitan song by
E. Nicolardi and E. De Curtis)

---

* If this voice wakens you in the night / as you clasp your husband close to you /
stay awake, if you want to stay awake / but pretend to be fast asleep.

My love,

I found out by chance that you are still alive. The greengrocer in the Sharia Farassa is an old man with Italian grandparents who insists on mantaining ties with his country of origin, and he must subscribe to a daily newspaper, delivered to the shop, and then maybe he doesn't even read it, but uses it to wrap up the salad the next day. Once a week they run a few pages with news from the province, the one where we met, and I haven't forgotten, you know? I remember so well those avenues of cypresses we used to ride along on our bicycles, and certain fall mornings when a light blue mist would rise up from the copses of young oaks, and the cottages on the plain, and the first group of houses where your family lived, and your smile—and it's really very strange when it smiles up at me from a crumpled newspaper from which, on the table in my room, I'm taking out the fruit and vegetables, and I see that it's the same smile as forty years before, when you said to me: Bye, see you tomorrow.

The way things happen. And what determines their course: a trifle. On August evenings, at sunset, the maritime pines down our way catch fire, from the brilliant green of daytime they become first golden, and then rosy, and then brick red, perhaps it was for this reason that Saint Luxorius, in the place name, was transformed first into Ruxorius and thence into Rossore, which means "redness," sometimes false etymologies lead to the right conclusion. I thought of redness. And I thought of shame. I got off my bicycle, I felt my face aflame, like the colors of the stand of pines. Only a stone's throw away, after the avenue framed by a rounded wall, there stood the Ascolis' house: only Luciana was still there, with her younger cousin, but their uncle and aunt had not returned. And by then three years had passed since the nightmare had ended, we all knew the fate that had befallen them, so why carry on waiting?, and why hadn't I gone there anymore to say something to them: a good evening, a syllable? I know what you would have replied: sure, well then, take your aunt and uncle, why do you carry on waiting for your aunt and uncle?, you never talk about them, as if they had left home to go off on a trip and ought to be back any minute. Because I do, I would have said to you, because I do, because it was all so absurd, so intolerably absurd that I too pretended like all the others that our relatives would have returned the following day; we even managed to laugh at the laws of that ugly little dwarf disguised as an emperor and we made up our jokes about them, and we thought: anyhow nothing's going to happen to us, these characters are just vulgar little monsters with their chests puffed out; we have culture, tradition, and some cash too. And instead, in a split second, they all disappeared. I thought: I'll go in, I won't go in, I'll go in, I won't go in, as if I were plucking the petals of a daisy. I didn't go in. In the meantime I had smoked about ten Giubeks, I crushed out the butts under the sole of my shoe, got back on my bicycle and went back to my place, where there was no one waiting for me and where I no longer waited for anyone.

My love, forgive me if I still call you the way I called you then, after all these years, but I really don't know what to call you. How should you address the woman you loved who said bye see you tomorrow and whom you abandoned without even leaving her a note to explain? For you have been my love all my life, and my woman too, because the few women I have had were furtive encounters for the gratification of the flesh, and instead every night, when I was trying to get to sleep, embracing the air around me in my solitary bed, I would call you my love, and the fact of thinking I was holding you in my arms always struck me as a great privilege. I remember the first night of escape, in Naples, in the little boarding house that was my first refuge; in the dark I would sing very softly *Voce 'e notte*, as if by singing that song in the dark my voice could reach you with the wish that you might find your honest husband, a man who loved you and who would embrace you at night and in whose embrace you might forget the pain I had caused you, and that he might be a good person, and without sins, and an innocent, and that he might not be anyone's victim, because, finally, by dint of seeing myself as a victim, I was no longer innocent, and with you I had behaved like the guiltiest of the guilty, and the basest.

But yesterday I saw you again in the greengrocer's newspaper, and all that I have spent my time burying, day after day, year after year, with the patience of geological eras, all that slow toil of mine vanished into nothingness as if by magic, or better, as if a bottomless pit made of time had opened up beneath my feet and I had sunk into it and joined you, because there is no resisting a photograph in a crumpled newspaper stained with salad. I dusted off the film of earth that covered your eyes and I too returned there, where you are. That photograph is beautiful, because it is honest, in the sense that it respects all the years that have gone by and it includes the generations that those years symbolize and represent. It portrays you in profile, holding a sheet of paper that you are apparently reading, because I know you, you always knew what to say, with your clear mind you don't need to read. Beside you is your grandson; according to the caption, he is called Sebastian and he plays the organ, as befits his name. He is a handsome boy, with prominent cheekbones and curly hair, and he looks so much like you, and I'd very much like to embrace him, because he reminds me of you when you were a little girl, and how I'd like it if he were my grandson, ours, the son of the son I did not generate with you. In the article, which is elegantly written, it says that he performed on the organ the concerto that Carl-Philip Emmanuel Bach composed in 1762 called *Solo for Harp*, and that the public was moved. How strange things are: perhaps this is why I found the courage to write you: because your grandson played on the organ that solo for harp that I played only for you on my harp, on the lawn of a country house, one evening in 1948, when a new August moon was about to rise. And with your smile, that evening's concerto (with the moon rising behind the cherry tree) resounds in the air, heads toward the low hills, rebounds off them, returns, skims us on the way back, and dissolves among the sounds of nature together with the breeze that lightly ruffles the leaves. Look, you murmur very quietly, a storm is coming, I hear it coming from the plain; leave off playing your instrument, my little David, respect the power of the elements. We have enjoyed the same notes and I put away my instrument and we sit looking at the blaze flaring up on the horizon, waiting for it to calm down, like the blood that —after having circulated too fast—explodes inside our body and needs a break. And in the silence transmitted to me by the photo in the newspaper I observe the audience that can be made out in front of you. Your sons and your husband are sitting in the front row; they have the happy look of those destined to have a good mother and a good wife, and from the smiles hovering on the faces of the public you understand that you have also been a good patroness to our community; this is why they pay tribute to you, for the things you have done. And so in the photograph in the greengrocer's newspaper I understood your life and I thought I would have you understand mine. How can you recount a life that took on the semblance of death, hiding itself away from life? It's impossible, I told myself, perhaps you can only recount the where, but never the why and the wherefore. Besides, my wherefore is the one you have always known, a wherefore of sounds, which are the notes I have always obtained from my instrument. And these notes were granted me only on some evenings, not every evening, because it wasn't easy in the early days, and what's more it never has been. The year I went away, your country, which I would have liked to consider mine too, believed it was reborn to a new life. And what an effervescence there was in the air! And what enthusiasm! They were going to vote, after many years, just imagine, and this made them feel enthusiastic and vigorous; they didn't just feel they had survived, they actually felt reborn, always a fine illusion. In the meantime I had arrived in Naples and I had taken a room in a boarding house in a working-class neighborhood. It was my first *where*, but I'll spare you that. But I do want to tell you that Naples is the most beautiful city in the world. Not so much for the city in itself, which is beautiful like many others perhaps, but for the people, who are truly the most beautiful in the world. My street was home to greengrocers, fishmongers, and small-time hoods. But these people were those things only during the day, because when evening fell and the hectic hustle and bustle of petty commercial and criminal dealings died down, they all stopped being greengrocers or fishmongers, or small-time hoods and they thought only of nostalgia, as if in a previous life they had been different people, or as if in a hypothetical future life they might become people different than greengrocers, fishmongers or hoods. They would pull out chairs from their wretched homes in the slums, the *bassi*, as they are known in Naples, and contemplating the alleyways and their grimy geometry the way one might look at the horizon, someone would begin to hum a melody, but softly, in the throat, for example *Voce 'e notte*, and that somebody would be joined by other voices, and it was a kind of prayer sung in chorus until one voice soared above the others and you heard for example "luntane 'e te quanta melanculia," far from you how melancholy I am, but

111

that melancholy was not all theirs, it was also the melancholy that their fathers or grandfathers had felt on leaving for the Americas, and they felt it in someone else's place, as if it were an inheritance that cannot be refused, which makes you feel its burden of suffering all the more. I would accompany them on the harp, which in the evenings I left with the greengrocer, the one who sang with the finest voice. He was chubby and ugly, he even had a squint, and maybe that was why nature had compensated him with that voice. Then, on Saturdays, I would put on my tails and go off to take my place in the orchestra of the great theater in that city, and in front of me, as the conductor waved his baton, I would see an elegant audience, with the gentlemen in dinner jackets and the ladies in long dresses, who were listening to that magic that only music can give, a magic that makes you forget the ugliness of the world. In that magnificent theatre full of stucco and gilt work, for whose orchestra I was the harpist Barucco (I chose this name for myself, I'm sure you like it), I never performed a solo. Yet I did my bit, for example Castelnuovo-Tedesco's concertino for harp with string quartet and clarinets, which we played when the theatre reopened after its restoration. And then there was the quintet for harp, flute, clarinet, saxophone and guitar by Villa-Lobos, which was moreover the piece that in some way succeeded in making us gel as an orchestra. I mean to say as an orchestra in formation, because every week a different orchestra would arrive; hunger was still making the rounds, many of us still had holes in our shoes, yet there was music. I didn't decide to leave until four years later. And not because I didn't love that city, which as I told you I loved with all my heart, but because I got the idea of taking . . . I really wouldn't know how to put it . . . well, a sort of census. A census of what?, you will ask me. Well, not really a census, but a sort of inspection, an absurd inspection, like someone seeking tracks in the snow after a blizzard. A flautist had told me that the orchestra of Salonika was looking for a flute and a harp, which are fairly uncommon instruments. He had a wife and children in Naples, and he stayed. I went.

Salonika is a city like Naples, it's not extraordinarily beautiful but, like Naples, it is full of people with beautiful spirits. Then again it's also beautiful as a city, because you have to discover its beauties. For example that section of the port where the seafront ends and you leave the central districts with the cafés and the restaurants, where Salonika breaks up into the fishermen's shacks, cordage and oil warehouses of the Ladadika district, and where you already feel poised between the Mediterranean, the Balkans and the Orient, amid a mélange of people made up of fishermen, day laborers, vagabonds, and people passing through, where it seems as if the Moors and Phidias have mixed. This is why mixtures are beautiful, because you can merge in with them without anyone looking for you, asking you who you are or why you are there. And that's what I did, changing my name to Baruckos. I let it be known that I was an Italian from Alexandria, and I didn't speak Greek, although I was learning it bit by bit.

It was in Salonika that for the first time they had me perform Hindemith's *Sonata*; the conductor was called Stavros, he was an old gentleman with a wooden leg and he used to hold the baton the way you hold a spaghetti fork, but maybe he was faking it, because he conducted splendidly; and as for me, that evening my fingers slipped over the strings as if they were flying, and I didn't realize I was playing, it was the harp that was playing itself. It was a success in its own way, and I think that Madame Ioanna still has the clippings from the newspapers of the day that came out with rave reviews, perhaps also because Hindemith was a composer in disfavor with the Nazis, who had spent his life in exile. So, the following week, after the big Beethoven concert, the maestro asked me to perform Villa-Lobos's *Concerto for Harp*. And the enthusiasm was so enormous that people got to their feet, the applause went on and on; Greek audiences are like that, they get enthusiastic, they wouldn't let me leave, the conductor asked me to play another piece of my choice, any one I wished. I had prepared the *Sonata* written by Casella in 1943; it is a haunting piece, it's something that seems to evoke the dead, a pity Casella was such a fascist, his art doesn't deserve that. The concert was held in the rotunda of the Byzantine church of Aghios Gheorgios, which is one of the extraordinary places of this world, because it gives you a sense of the sacred even if you don't believe in the sacred. But that audience knew what the sacred is: their war had only just finished, and too many had died. And I saw that the people in the front rows, not only the women, but also the old folks, were weeping, no sound came from the city, the only sound was the harp, and it seemed to be protecting the survivors, and almost without my noticing it, from Casella's chords my fingers slipped into an old Greek song called *Thaxanarthis*, which means "You will return," and the public began to murmur the words, yet they didn't seem like human voices, it was as if the earth and the sea and all the nature surrounding us were breathing with us and, in breathing, were singing. Then I stopped playing and the song stopped too; we all got up in silence, the women made the sign of the cross in the Orthodox manner and we went out into the night of Salonika, each toward his own home.

My home in Salonika for all those years was the Petros boarding house. It was in Ladadika, beyond the oil and cordage warehouses that later became frozen fish and fuel storehouses. When I arrived there, in my first days in Greece, I saw a woman cementing over the bullet holes in the façade. She had our profile, beautiful hair and a face marked by life. I spoke to her in French and she didn't understand. I didn't want to speak Italian and a strange intuition prompted me to say "Estó buscando un lugar por dormer," and she answered me in Ladino, or *sefarditika* as they call it there, and she asked me where I was from. From nothingness, I replied. Then there is a room for you here, said she, I am Ioanna, I need someone to help me patch up this house that my Petros built.

From the room I always occupied you can see the sea and, farther on, to the right, the mountains of Chalcidice with their suggestion of the Orient. I spent entire nights at that window, looking at the distant mountains on which fires were being lit and thinking again of a meadow in front of a house on the edge of the maquis, of a night, and of the music I played there. My bed had a metal headboard painted with an Arcadian scene showing a shepherd with ankles swathed in white cloth who is playing his pipe for a herd of goats. On the wall above the bed there was a reproduction of a Byzantine Christ that a naïve painter had recopied during the previous century for the peasants or fisherfolk of these parts. In front of the bed there was a bureau in which I kept my linen and beside that stood the wardrobe in reddish cherrywood where I always used to hang up my tails; it had a mirror blotched with sandy flecks in which I always did the best I could to avoid my image. I didn't play in Salonika only: we also went to Alexandropolis, Athens, Patras, and Belgrade too, on what was an important occasion for Europe, I think, or at least that's what the papers said. The program was not very demanding, for my instrument: we played obvious music, by great musicians, or at least it was obvious for me. Only on certain occasions were lesser known compositions reserved for me, like Migot's *Sonate liuthée* or Fauré's *Impromptu*, because I asked the conductor to ring the changes a bit. That evening, I remember well, we were in the theater of Dionysus, beneath the Parthenon; by way of an audience we had French tourists unloaded from two blue and white buses, they were looking for something typically Greek and they found decadent music, and I thought of giving them some real decadence, not that artificial stuff churned out to evoke emotions on the cheap, but the sublime variety, the kind Migot and Fauré knew how to make.

Ioanna would come to visit me three times a year: on her birthday, on Orthodox Easter Day and on her wedding anniversary. She would push the door slightly ajar, without knocking. Petros, are you sleeping?, she would murmur in the dark. No, I would reply, I was here at the window, I have a touch of insomnia. And what is my Petros thinking of?, she would ask me slipping into bed. Of a farmhouse, I replied, of music on an evening when a summer storm broke.

On Saturdays I would roam around the city looking at the names on the doorbells, by then they were no longer the names of our people, not even of those who had borne Greek names for centuries. Sometimes, very seldom, I would ring the bell. To find whom?, you will ask me. Yes, to find whom: a woman alone, some old survivors, strangers who wondered what I was looking for or for whom? Did I perhaps take myself for that David whose task was to take a census of the tribes of Israel? And what kind of census was mine, if I may call it that? Was I collecting shadows perhaps? Yes, that's it, at bottom I spent twenty years collecting shadows, that's what I did in Salonika. It almost seemed to me as if I had a bottomless basket in which I collected the notes I played on concert evenings. Is it perhaps possible to collect musical notes? It's not, they vanish back to where they came from, into the air, because air is what they are made of.

When I left Salonika for Alexandria, Ioanna wanted to carry my bags to the steamer. I had objected because women mustn't serve men, but she called a cab, like a great lady, and she put on a little hat with a veil. I don't know if it was the hat she wore on her wedding day, but this is unimportant. She said to me: Chrisostomos, I have loved you through a veil and through a veil I bid you farewell. And then she said in our language: "Va a la bon hora, el Dios que sé con ti." I can still see her in the back of the harbor waving farewell with her hand, a wave she then transformed into two arms held outstretched, like one who yields in the face of evidence of the life before which both had yielded for some time. I had called myself Chrisostomos when I arrived in Greece, and Chrisostomos I stayed on the posters and programs of the orchestra in Alexandria. Which wasn't really an orchestra, because at first it was a quartet: a harp, a flute, an oboe, and a cello. But this didn't happen until later. At first I went off alone, because in an ad in a Salonika newspaper I had read that the Hôtel Cecil was looking for an instrumentalist to entertain the guests at cocktail hour. A classical instrument and classical music, it specified. I sent a telegram: solo harpist classical performer. The contract too was arranged by telegram.

At the end of the fifties Alexandria was already the devastated city it is now, but the so-called "beau monde" still frequented the two luxury hotels: the Windsor Palace and the Hôtel Cecil. After a test piece in the presence of the manager, a little Frenchman from Marseilles who pretended he understood music, we agreed on a reasonable salary, meals included. They also offered me, in the servants' quarters, an attic room furnished like a doll's house that in the fifties had been home to the chef, who was apparently renowned. The view was most beautiful, and then they proudly showed me rooms once occupied by Somerset Maugham and Winston Churchill, but I stayed there only one week, the time it took to find myself a room in the kind of boarding house I like, the room where I am now writing you. Certain hotels are strange: you get the feeling that the famous personages who patronized them left their unhappiness there, and people like me who have chosen to disappear prefer the anonymous unhappiness left by anonymous types like ourselves who frequented the same room and looked at their anonymous faces in the same blotchy mirror above the washbasin. And so, even though the Corniche in Alexandria has a certain blowsy charm, I chose to stay out of the picture. I found myself a little boarding house in the Sharia-al-Nabi district, right behind the Temple, which was built by the Italians, one of the rare good things that the Italians have done for us, even though the architecture isn't up to much, what with that gaudy pink marble.

I carried on playing in the Hôtel Cecil for seven years. Seven years is a lot, but it wasn't servitude, because Cecil wasn't Laban and I didn't have to play the shepherd. In the evenings I used to wear a rather threadbare dinner jacket (the tails were for truly special occasions) provided by the hotel, and I would entertain the guests for three hours, from 5:30 to 8:30, as they took tea or an aperitif. In the course of those evenings I would play mostly accessible composers, suited to the public and the place: a very romantic sonatina by Hoffmann, the *Grande etude à l'initiation de la mandoline* by Parish-Alvars and Ravel's *Allegro for harp*, which is definitely accessible but by way of compensation is also extremely beautiful. True, the six instruments Ravel called for were missing, but one does what one can, and the audience settled for that. Besides, the audience was often made up of inattentive people who were there to chat, to see, and to be seen. Every so often, around eight, when an orange light that immediately turns into indigo falls over Alexandria, between one classical piece and the next, I would play the chords of *Voce 'e notte*, trying to coax from the arpeggio a sound that was as far removed as possible from the harmonic functions, and that created a strange atmosphere, like an indefinable magic; the clients seemed rapt, perhaps moved, I saw that the champagne glasses were motionless in midair and the waiters set down on the tables their trays full of pieces of *bouri* stuck on toothpicks.

When I got a job with the symphony orchestra I decided to have my name entered among the list of the musicians as

Chrisostomos and no more, because it was the name I felt belonged to me most. And I can say without false modesty that my debut was a triumph. The first times I only had to play chords, as is often the harpist's lot in symphony music, but that evening was entirely for me, because the program included Mozart's *Concerto for harp, flute and orchestra*, among the most beautiful things ever written for a harpist, and perhaps for music *tout court*. The orchestra was magnificent, the flautist was of a good caliber, but Mozart reserved the best part for the harp, and Chrisostomos did not miss his chance.

And so the years went by. Normal people don't notice, and the years go by for them too, but without their noticing. Of memorable things for me, as far as I can tell you, there was a trip to Abu Simbel with the orchestra because it was, they said, a truly exceptional day; we were to play for that great world organization that had raised the funds for the restoration of the ancient temples. And in fact there were many important personalities that evening, seated among the millennial stones. It was a most beautiful night and there was a moon. I was free to play the pieces I wished, and so I began with Debussy's *Sacred and Profane Dances*. And then, after a brief interval, I performed my *Solo for Harp*. Maybe it's not a sublime piece, but for me it has a significance that it perhaps doesn't have for others and for me that night it was sublime, down there in the desert. You know, in the desert, at night, if there is a moon, the sand glitters like the sea and seems made of silver. And I thought of our house, and of you, as I played. And for the first time since I had disappeared I stopped thinking that obsessive thought, that phrase that had made me run away and had always resounded in my head: what's the use of a harp with only one string when all the others are broken? I don't know why I stopped thinking it, I don't know why this happened. The way things happen. And what determines their course: a trifle. It was night in the desert, the sand was glittering beneath the moon, I was playing my harp and it seemed to me that the grains of sand that surrounded me, the audience and the temples, began to respond to the sound. As if those grains of sand, millions and millions of them, had awoken from a long sleep and were responding to me: I caressed a chord in C minor and they responded to me, I plucked a flat and they responded; those voices were alive, that evening, it's completely absurd but that's the way it was, they were resuscitated from the crematorium ovens in which they had been annihilated.

After that I went on no more trips, not any more. I stayed here, in my boarding house, in this room of mine. By now I no longer play in the orchestra, I'm too old; only sometimes, exceptionally, if a harpist falls sick or doesn't arrive in the capital for some reason, for these days harpists have become difficult as prima donnas. It's an austere room, you know this yourself. On the right there is a mirror, and then a bed where many dreams of love have been dreamt. The newspaper that brought you back to me says that soon you will be invited to this country; it is a tribute that two stupidly hostile sister communities are making to you as the woman of peace you are. This is good, because it crowns the dream of your life, which certainly has been full of sense. I won't be in the audience, but if I am it will be as if I weren't. But it can happen that the sense of someone's life is, senselessly, simply this: to seek vanished voices, and maybe one day to believe that he has found them, on a day that this someone no longer expected, one evening when he is old and tired and playing beneath the moon, collecting all the voices that come from the sand. And, he thinks, this is no miracle, for we don't need miracles, we leave them to others, gladly. And so, you think, perhaps it's only an illusion, a wretched illusion, which nevertheless for a moment, as long as you have played that music, was really true. But you lived your life only for that, and you feel that this gives a sense to senselessness, don't you think?

A Good Man like You

Some things are in our power,
others are not in our power. In our power are
opinion, sentiment, aversion

(EPICTETUS, *Manual*)

My dear,

" . . . because things can't go on like this, for me, perhaps you didn't realize, but I have the right to think of myself, and so save myself. Some nights I used to think: what am I, to him?, a refuge, a hearth, a comfort? And how is it possible that I come after everything else, I mean really *everything*? As you know, I love you (or perhaps I loved you), but put yourself in my shoes, you who are so good at putting yourself in the shoes of those who are suffering, try at least once to put yourself in my shoes. Sure, what you do is noble, I don't wish to deny that, and if there were a paradise you would deserve it, even though you maybe believe in it less than I do. And I understand that you feel the sufferings of the world upon your shoulders, but look, you aren't the one who's going to cure them, the world has always suffered and it will suffer still, despite the existence of people like you. Take your last trip to Abyssinia for example. Leaving like that, in twenty-four hours, while I was in Venice at my mother's place, just because your Organization had sent you a telegram from Paris requesting your urgent departure. You called me from the airport, at the last minute, as you were boarding, I don't know if you realize. Do you really think this is the way to do things? You said to me: look at the photographs they sent me from Paris and you'll understand everything, I left them for you on the bureau at the front door. And the first thing I did as soon as I got back from Venice (you obliged me to take the 16:41 train that changes in Bologna at 18:48 and gets home at 19:47, though you know that Venice is far away and that I like to stay overnight, to avoid unreasonably long round trips in one day) was to look at your terrible photographs. You could see a parched plain, ground cracked by the drought, a bunch of people beneath tarpaulins, women with babies in their arms, creatures with distended bellies and bulging eyes. I can imagine how it makes you feel good to get off your organization's airplane, unload crates of foodstuffs, set up the field hospital, put on the white coat and the sterilized gloves you brought with you from Europe, and in the light of lamps powered by generators practice your redeeming arts on the poor bodies of those children. I can understand this, I repeat. But you must understand me too. I threw those horrible photos in the trash and took the first train back to my mother's. There was no way I was going to wait for you at home like Penelope, in the state of mind I found myself in. Gianni, as you know, has always been kind not only to me, but also to you, even though he doesn't know you, because he esteems you as a person, and I'm sure that a good man like you will manage to understand all that . . ."

Look, it would be downright pointless for you to go on, truly, my dear, for you know, I understand you the way no one else can, but I want to let you go on, because it's also true that a detailed explanation will make you feel lighter, less subject to a guilt that I really don't want you to feel. There is absolutely no doubt about Giannikins' kindness, and certainly none about his civic sense: that was the first thing I understood. And the fact that he would give you a little call in the morning and the evening, Come on don't take it bad, Come on don't let it get you down, and other things of that sort that cheer you up and make you feel like a person, is a fact that touches me, because it means that someone was looking after you, something you needed extremely badly in that accursed period. I understand perfectly when you tell me about that day when you had decided to spend the weekend in our old house by the sea, and at a certain point you stopped at the edge of the road, turned off the engine and, as you put it, you "seized up." Do you know what happened? I'll tell you. In psychiatric terms it's called "panic." You simply had a panic attack. Not that in certain cases of panic one ought to overlook the psychological causes, naturally: in your case, precisely the fact that you were in the grip of great anxiety. Because, as you tell me, the knowledge that you would find that house deserted, that I was far away, as if vanished into thin air, gave you a profound feeling of desertion, or better, of dejection. And what's the point of doing something like that, one wonders without wondering about it, in other words where's the sense in going off to spend the weekend in a house where I have spent happy days with a person if now that person is no longer there, and everything, the furniture, the objects, even the plates, speak of him to me? You don't need to have the goodness you attribute to me to understand something like that: anyone would understand it. Just as I am the first to realize just how close Giannikins has been to you. At bottom I am grateful to him for that, you know?, and I understand how he could constitute a point of reference for you. Well, that day, you were telling me, you had a panic attack, even though in reality the expression is mine. Luckily there was that café, on the other side of the road, the place that doubles as a general store, run by that old man with the wooden leg who is something of an institution in our little seaside village. You left the car below the old house with the plaque where the trumpeter poet was born, you managed to go inside, you called Giannikins. Do you perhaps think that I don't know why you called Giannikins? And whom were you supposed to call?— me perhaps, who in that moment was in Abyssinia?—because that day I actually was in Abyssinia.

Gianni is a man of good sense, and experienced, and above all he loves you (he loves us both). He told you what a person who loves you could tell you, as you put it in your letter: friendly, soothing, affectionate words. The ones you needed to hear. For in life we always need to hear the words we want to hear, and Gianni, thank heaven, understood perfectly which words you needed to hear. And thanks to his words you managed to get back into the car and make it as far as our house, which is less than a mile from the village; you drove through the olive grove (by the way, have those money-grubbing new proprietors already torn it up and transformed it into a vineyard?) and finally you went into the house. You threw open the doors and windows and, as you say in the letter, the house didn't strike you as inhabited by ghosts, the feeling of my absence did not seem so distressing, you fixed yourself some tea, slipped on a sweater, and you realized that things weren't as frightening as you had thought, and that despite everything life goes on.

And the rest, over and above what you tell me, I can imagine by myself. I appreciate, however, your telling me, with great altruism, that it must make quite an impression on a man to return home after an absence, even though rather a long one, to find—not his woman—but a letter on the bureau instead. And I don't deny that it did make a certain impression on me, because in my heart (how foolish I am, eh?), that day, as I was coming home after a murderous flight, I was thinking of inviting you to dinner at Esiodo, you know, the old trattoria where you eat bread soup and broiled steak, and I was sure that, over dinner, you would have asked me: how did it go?, how are you?, did you suffer? And instead a man finds a letter in which he is told that he will certainly understand the situation, good man that he is. And, as I was telling you, I understood, even though you must allow me to tell you that regarding my goodness you are exaggerating, because I'm not as good as you say, besides, and maybe I'm wrong, in your defining me as good there has always been a hint of superiority, I don't dare say contempt.

Anyway, look . . . I imagined the rest perfectly well, and there was really no need for you to tell me. The following week Gianni made you a gift of a cell phone (one of the first!) and told you: When you are in trouble, call me. Naturally he gave you instructions on how to call him with the due precautions, because a man of his age married for over thirty years to a second wife must always take his precautions, and this too is understandable. But in any case we all know that when a man says he is happily married he is talking about monotony, in fact let's be frank: his marriage is on the rocks. Besides, despite his age, Gianni is still a handsome man. And above all he knows how to pay court. Not that stupid courtship that people normally mean when they talk about courtship: but the genuinely affectionate attentions of one who really cares, one who wants to know how a woman is feeling, how she passes her day, how she sleeps. And one fine day—this too is understandable, but you could have done without writing this —you invited him to our house by the sea. You called him on the cell phone he had given you and you said: Giannino, thanks to you and your support I managed to get home here among the olives, and I'd like to invite you to dinner. And he didn't wait to be asked twice.

You know, throughout your letter, which is so sincere and met with my most sincere understanding, there's something wrong. Perhaps it may strike you as odd, or an insignificant detail, but it's where you tell me you responded to a request for affection. Or rather, that you responded to a request for love. A love is requited when both parties are in love, my dear, and I expected you to write this to me, with that great faithfulness that has always characterized our life. You could have (should have) told me: you know, while you were away I chanced to fall in love. A little or a lot is immaterial, because there are various degrees of love, just as there are of fever: it may be a mild fever or a high fever, but it is in any event a rise in temperature. But no, you pass off your Giannikins like this, as if he were a refreshment. As if to say: you know, you weren't around, and in the meantime I got myself some refreshment. By the way, I read in an anthropology text that on the Cantabrian coast, a place from which people have emigrated throughout history and especially a place with ports where men took ship as sailors and stayed far from home for long stretches, there was a time when, in order to avoid spells of sadness and loneliness, those women bereft of their men would find themselves a good man to keep them company, and that's exactly what these characters were called: a "refreshment." It's not that they lived together, nor did they raise a new family, nothing of the sort, they simply went together until the grass widow's real husband returned. Who's that fellow who's making time with that woman? people would wonder. Him? He's Maria's or Juanita's refreshment. It was an accepted fact in society, and it scandalized nobody. Now, I don't wish to deny that Giannikins was your "refreshment" for the first two or three months. Besides, he must be good at refreshing: he's had two wives and three or four fiancées, and maybe in life he has thought of nothing else but refreshing ladies who had gotten a little hot. But you will grant me that if a man returns to his home after seven months and instead of his woman he finds a letter waiting for him on the bureau, he has the right to think that it is not merely a question of a refreshment. Especially if in that letter he is told why. Well, listen, there's no point in your continuing with this letter of yours—so detailed and so logical—and there's no point in your telling me for the umpteenth time: a good man like you cannot fail to understand that I had to fill up my solitude, and that at bottom I did so for us, because this affair with Gianni is an impossible love, given his family situation and his age: it is a way, at bottom, of waiting for you, for in any case this absurd love affair with him could not go any farther, even those lady friends of mine who have been closest to me throughout this business tell me this, although Loretta said: Why not?, for the time being enjoy this love affair, then we'll see; he's a charming man, and above all he's so solid in ideological terms. A good man like me, to use your expression, would understand. And I understood. I understood perfectly well. I understand that two people in your situation can leave for the falls of Iguazu. Brazil is a fascinating country, I know that too, you know that I worked in Amazonia and in the Northeast; it's a virgin country, immense, the ideal place in which to make a new life, and to see the world too, especially for a person like you, to whom I used to talk about the world because she stayed at home. And what if one fine day Gianni, yes, this very Gianni, who has never worked as an engineer in his life, because he thought he was a great erotic poet, if, I was saying, if this very Gianni were actually invited by the National Office for Developing Countries to supervise a great engineering project in that distant country, were you perhaps supposed to let him leave too, now that finally there was someone who took you with him not to deserts, among exhausted people and malnourished children, but to a luxuriant part of the globe, to stay in a first-class hotel right next to the construction site, with a fabulous salary for him, and you treated like a princess, the way you never have been treated in your life? And again, if Gianni had made you a sordid proposal, to you who has always had a gypsy spirit, if for example he had said to you: Listen, dear, I have a nice house in Venice, which is moreover a romantic city, where we could see each other at weekends, we could have some really affectionate encounters, in the meantime you could even visit your mother; you take your train, easy as pie, I take mine from Milan and we'll be there in practically the same time; the important thing is that my wife doesn't get to hear of it, you know, she's even four or five years younger than you, I threw away my first marriage for her, and all things considered I love her, I have grandchildren through my first wife and children with this one, you will understand that at my age I don't feel like making a new life a third time. Listen, if he had said that to you I realize that you would have told him to go to hell, with the pride that I recognize in you, there's no doubt that you would have said: Giannino, take a drive down the road to the train station one evening, you'll find the right kind of woman for you. But he, what with the situation he finds himself in, with his position, and with his pretty wife, who between you and me is by no means your inferior, stakes everything on an *amour fou* that I truly never thought him capable of. And what else could you have done but follow him to Iguazu? I have to say, and forgive me the rather comical paradox, that I would have gone too. Oh!, if only there had been a Giannikins in my life.

Instead I found Giovanna. Who also loves me. And I love her. She's naïve all right, I don't deny it, but you have to consider her age; at bottom compared to you she is a youngster, something that you and I, my dear, have not been for some time, and she wanted a child with me and she managed, something that we didn't manage. Of course she doesn't have your qualities, your élan, your initiative, and above all your bohemian attitude. In life she is above all a philologist, in the sense that she sifts every word, every situation. Just think, when she came to our house, the first thing she said was: We'll need to redo the parquet here. She isn't a complicated woman, her world is wholly bound up with the beautiful things we now have, without existential anxieties or worries about success. I assure you that her greatest satisfaction was redoing the parquet. But at least she doesn't get worked up, and if I go off for a few months she doesn't moan at me, she doesn't feel like a poor outcast as may happen to certain women who cannot live without a man for more than a week.

It was by pure chance that I found out that you and Gianni had returned. The dam is finished, and it was time for both of you to return, I found this out by chance from Gianni's doctor, who as you know is a dear friend of mine. He too would like to work as a doctor for the United Nations, because he is generous and has a big heart, but his little wife keeps him on a tight leash, with the pretext that she cannot give up her job.

And so you mustn't be surprised if after seven years I am recopying the letter you left me on the bureau, moreover I'm sure I'm doing you a favor, because you certainly didn't have the time to make a rough draft, given the haste with which you left me. True, it's been a long time, and it'll certainly strike you as strange to receive a recopied version of your letter of seven years ago, but you know, life repeats itself. And I thought: What am I to do now with her letter, given that her race is run, at least the one with Gianni. You know, yesterday I dropped in on Dr. Baudino, my dear friend whose laboratory deals in tropical diseases. I knew that on his return Gianni was worried about having picked up an amoeba or some similar illness, but it's not that I was particularly worried about that. My friend wasn't in, it seems that he had gone off to celebrate his silver wedding anniversary with the amoebas, because he has been working with tropical diseases for over twenty years now. His secretary was there, a good but ingenuous girl. She says to me: the doctor isn't in, you won't catch him until tomorrow. No matter, I say, I'll sit down in his office for a moment, to take a quick look at his records, which are mine too at the end of the day.

Gianni's test results were in plain view. It's a sarcoma, my dear, a sarcoma of the prostate. I don't know if you are aware of this, maybe you're not, but sarcoma is one of the most aggressive forms of cancer, it spreads immediately, and in fact I believe that Gianni is already in metastasis. Sooner or later my friend Baudino will have to tell you this, because it's pointless his kidding you with the excuse about a tropical disease when we're looking at something quite different. But perhaps, poor devil, who knows what qualms about human respect he will have about informing you of this; he knows that you sacrificed a marriage for Gianni, that you put your life on the line for him, that you immolated yourself for him, and that you are no longer in the first flush of youth. And so, good man as I am, I thought I would let you know, for after all I am still your friend. When you go into complete metastasis, the pain gets very bad, really very bad, and Gianni will howl like a dog. And you will be terrified, because the cries of someone who is that sick are the worst kind you can possibly hear. And in a country like ours, where pain therapy is taken into absolutely no account, they'll really make him suffer like a dog, because the doctors are afraid to fall foul of the law if they prescribe doses of morphine in excess of those permitted. Should this happen, as I think it will, do come to me. I have two suitcases full of morphine, with which I travel the world, and I can supply you with some without any problems. But maybe you should let me know before the end of December, because then Giovanna and I are planning to make a long trip to Mexico and we probably won't be back until late spring. We're going to do the whole of the Yucatan, and we might even go as far as Guatemala.

Books Never Written,
Journeys Never Made

Allons! Whoever you are come travel with me!
Traveling with me you find what never tires.

(WALT WHITMAN, *Leaves of Grass*)

Na vespera de não partir nunca
ao menos não há que arrumar malas. *

(FERNANDO PESSOA, *Poems of Alvaro de Campos*)

* On the eve of never departing / at least you don't have to pack your bags.

My love,

Do you remember when we didn't go to Samarkand? We chose the best season of the year, the beginning of autumn. The woods and the bushes around Samarkand, where the sun-baked hills descend and the vegetation begins, become a blaze of red and yellow ocher leaves, and the climate is mild, said our guidebook; do you remember our guidebook? We had bought it in a little bookstore in the Île Saint-Louis, Ulysse, specializing in travel books, mostly secondhand and often underlined or annotated by the people who had made those journeys, leaving notes in their guidebooks, highly useful notes too, like: "inn recommended," or "road to be avoided, dangerous," or "in this emporium they sell fine carpets at affordable prices," or "watch out, in this restaurant they chisel you on the check."

You can get to Samarkand in a variety of ways, said the guide, and the fastest is by air, but this is certainly the most banal way to go. For example you can leave from Paris, Rome, or Zurich and fly direct to Moscow, but you have to spend the night there because there is no connecting flight that allows you to reach Uzbekistan the same evening. And: was it worth spending the night in Moscow? We talked this over at length in Luigi's, that restaurant in the alley where you eat good fish and where there was a really nice homosexual waiter who served us exquisitely. For my part it was an idea I didn't feel like ruling out. Why not, I said, do you remember?, just think: Red Square at night seen from that big hotel that Aeroflot puts at the disposal of tourists who must spend the night in Moscow; it's autumn and it's already cold in Moscow, le place rouge will be empty as it is in Gilbert Becaud's song, I'll call you Nathalie, we'll get out of a cab—in the Soviet Union cabs are like limousines used by heads of state, I read somewhere—and in the hotel restaurant they'll offer us sturgeon caviar from the Volga, maybe there will already be a little fog around the lamps, as in Pushkin's novels, and it will be beautiful, I am sure; we might also go to the Bolshoi—it is obligatory to go when in Moscow—and maybe we'll see *Swan Lake.*

But it was the most banal choice, and so we both agreed to drop it. The journey overland, by train, was much preferable and that's why we decided: the Orient-Express and then either the Transiberian or via Teheran. The glamour of the Orient-Express works its magic on even the most snobbish intellectuals, and, while we were far from considering ourselves among their number, perhaps we were, and this is why we said: by train, by train. Oh, the train! Do you know that when Georges Nagelmackers thought of laying the track for his luxury express train he had to negotiate with France, Bavaria, Austria and Rumania, all of which felt that their national integrity was threatened ? The line was inaugurated in 1883, and the first journey was painstakingly described by Edmond About, the journalist and humorist who wrote *The Notary's Nose.* Nagelmackers would never have succeeded without the help of King Leopold II of Belgium, who was also his partner. And perhaps it will amaze you to know that back in those days certain locomotives exceeded a speed of one hundred miles per hour; they were British Buddicoms with a compressed-air braking system. Do you want to know the menu of January 4, 1898?, I got hold of it. Brace yourself because this was no snack: oysters for starters, along with turtle soup or *potage à la reine*; then salmon trout *à la Chambord*, saddle of venison *à la duchesse*, woodcock, *parfait de foie gras*, truffles in champagne, fruit and dessert. And then the couchettes, the rattling of the journey that during the night was muffled by the glass of the windows, as the train ran through towns and loved them without touching them, just as Chardonne used to say to his friends: "Si vous aimez une femme, n'y touchez pas," and the sleeping car, which allowed us to touch a town with our fingertips, like that poet who wanted to touch the movements of a harpist without touching her hands. I recited you poems about trains from memory, and in the bistro near the Gare d'Austerlitz I declaimed Valery Larbaud: "Oh, Orient-Express, lend me that vibrant chanterelle voice of yours, the light and easy breathing of slim locomotives that effortlessly draw four yellow wagons with gilded letters amid the mountainous solitude of Serbia and through rose-strewn Bulgaria . . . "

From where do you take the Orient-Express? The Gare de Lyon, from the Gare de Lyon! And in that marvelous station, what is there? The Train Bleu of course, the most charming restaurant in Paris! Do you remember it? Sure you remember it, you cannot not remember it. The Train Bleu has three enormous rooms with art pompier frescoes on the walls, couches in red plush, Bohemian chandeliers and waiters wearing spencers and immaculate aprons who say to you "Bienvenus, Messieurs Dames" with a couldn't-give-a-damn air. Just for starters we ordered oysters and champagne, because a couple who are not leaving for Samarkand on the Orient-Express have the right to start like this, don't they? Leaving is always a bit like dying we said, observing the people who would have remained on the platform talking and bidding farewell to the passengers leaning out from the illuminated windows. Wherever was that elderly bald gentleman going? The one with the dressy cravat who was smoking his pipe at the window with the same nonchalance as a man sitting in his own living room? And the lady sitting in the same carriage, with a crimson hat and a fur collar, was she his wife or just a stranger? And during the journey would they have an affair? Who knows, who knows, and so let the journey begin, we said; the train left from platform L, or at least that's what the departures board said, and the first stop would be Venice. Oh, Venice, how you had dreamed of seeing Venice!, the Grand Canal, San Marco, the Ca' d'Oro . . . Yes, dear, agreed, but I don't think you'll be able to see much of it, I'm truly sorry, but the train merely makes an overnight stop at Santa Lucia station, at most you'll see the lagoon over which the railroad runs, the lagoon to the left and the open sea to the right, but I wouldn't like you to forget that we are heading for Samarkand, otherwise you'll feel like stopping in all the cities the train the train passes through, first Vienna, then Istanbul, maybe you would like to see Istanbul?, just think, the Bosphorus, the mosques, the minarets, the Grand Bazaar.

In short, the real journey not to make was the one to Samarkand. I have an unforgettable memory of it, and such a clear one, as detailed as only the things experienced truly in the imagination can be. You know, I was reading a French philosopher who observed how the imagination obeys laws as strict as those of reality. And the imagination, my love, has nothing to do with the illusory, which is really another matter. Samuel Butler was really quite a character, not only for the fantastic novels that he wrote, but for the way he saw life. Something he wrote comes to mind: "I do not mind lying, but I hate inaccuracy." My love, we have told each other many lies in our lifetime, and we accepted all of them reciprocally, because they were really true things in our imagination of desire. But there was one, or, if you prefer, several lies clustered around the same real event, that left us lost for ever, because it was a false lie, because it was the illusory, and the illusory is necessarily inaccurate, it exists only in the fog of self-delusion. In our dreams we'd always acted like Don Quixote, who pushes his imagination all the way, an imagination that implies madness, provided that it is accurate: accurate in the topography of the real landscape that he crosses in his imagination. Have you ever thought that *Don Quixote* is a realistic novel? But instead, one day, from Don Quixote you suddenly become Madame Bovary, with her incapacity to delineate the contours of what she desired, to decipher the place in which she found herself, to count the money she spent, or to understand the fuck-ups she made: they were real things and to her they seemed like air, and not the opposite. What an enormous difference: you can't say "I went to a distant city," or "There was a thoughtful gentleman who kept me company," or "I don't think it was love, more a kind of tenderness." You can't say things like that, my love, or at least you couldn't say them to me, for that was your illusion, your poor pathetic illusion: that city had a precise name and it wasn't all that distant either, and he was only a man of a certain age with whom you went to bed. He was a lover of yours whom you thought was made of air, but who was made of flesh.

This is why I remind you of the journey we didn't make to Samarkand, because that was the one that was real and ours and full and lived. And so I'll continue our game. As that philosopher I was telling you about says, memory calls up lived experience, it is precise, exact, implacable, but it produces nothing new: that is its limitation. The imagination, however, cannot call up anything, because it cannot remember, and that is its limitation: but by way of compensation it produces the new, something that wasn't there before, that has never been there. This is why I have fallen back on these two faculties, memory and imagination, which can assist each other reciprocally, to call up once more the journey to Samarkand that we never made but imagined down to the slightest detail.

Our traveling companions were respectively disappointing and exciting. The extremely elegant gentleman who seemed so refined turned out to be a small-time businessman, somewhat on the venal side; we didn't manage to understand what kind of import-export trade he carried on with Turkey, but there was something shady about it, or at least you smelled a rat, you winked at me a couple of times, do you remember?; and when he got off at Istanbul you even heaved a sigh of relief, because his compliments to you were becoming excessively gallant for a stranger met on the train, and you were at your wit's end, while I made a show of indifference. But the lady turned out to be much better than her appearance promised. I mean to say: a Chekhovian look suited to the character, was the comment you whispered to me in the corridor. And in fact, I never saw a woman as Chekhovian as she. She began with the age of the little girl in "Sleepy." Up to what point can the physiological need for sleep have a bearing on a homicide? Oh, well, that depends, the charming lady expatiated with confidence; for example, have the lady and gentleman ever studied sleep, biologically speaking, I mean? Well, the waking state has a threshold of tolerability, a bit like pain, and this varies with age; for example there is an age at which the need for sleep is an irrepressible necessity that dominates all other sensations and necessities, especially in a person of the female gender, and that is the moment of early puberty, which is one of the reasons why the little servant girl suffocated the newborn baby girl whom she was supposed to look after and whose crying would not let her sleep: for that night, or at most the previous night, she had had her first menstruation, and she was exhausted.

I have given you a hasty and modest summary, because the lady, as you will recall better than I, had a really elegant vocabulary and fantastic descriptive capacities, and her competence on Chekhov was by no means limited to picturesque or erudite anecdotes like this one. Do you remember for example her discourse on Chekhov's last words? You must remember, we were both left astounded, and moreover neither you nor I knew that as he was dying Chekhov said "Ich sterbe." Right, he died in a language that wasn't his. Really strange, isn't it? He always loved in Russian, suffered in Russian, hated (a little) in Russian, smiled (a lot) in Russian, always lived in Russian and died in German. That unknown lady gave an extraordinary explanation of the fact that Chekhov had died in German, and when she bade us goodbye as she got off at an unknown station I will never forget the expression on your face: marvel, amazement, and maybe emotion. And how beautiful and extraordinary it was that day when I saw you running toward me. I was waiting for you in the same old café as ever, and you cut through the crowd with a happy air waving a little book in your hand and yelling: "Look who the old lady was!" The book had just come out and the critics hadn't noticed it yet, but it hadn't escaped you, nothing ever escaped you, oh, the delightful old lady, great and benevolent voice whose golden fruits had added such pleasure to our journey without revealing her identity before she vanished into nothingness. And the improper use that we made in Samarkand of Chekhov's last words! Naturally, I started it, and then you began to imitate me, even though at first you said: You're blasphemous, you are really blasphemous! The first time was in that kind of tower of Babel called Siab Bazaar: the smells, the spices, the headgear, the carpets, the bawling, the throng, the crowd that was a mixture of Turkistan, Europe, Russia, Mongolia and Afghanistan, and I stopped dumbfounded and yelled: "Ich sterbe!" And after that "to sterb" became a password, an obligation, almost a vice. We sterbed together before the mausoleum of Gur-i-Emir, that ceramic corn cob sitting atop the cylindrical tower engraved with verses from the Koran, the onyx of the internal panels, the jade tombstone trimmed with arabesques and marked with the yellow and green of the tiles. We sterbed more than ever in Raghistan Square, with its two turreted madrassehs before which a crowd was prostrate in prayer. The binoculars that we took with us were indispensible: that had been your advice, in practical things you were unbeatable at times. Without them we would have never deciphered the ceramic mosaics that decorate the courtyard of the Ulug Beg mosque, that pattern with flowers of twenty petals inscribed within a twelve-pointed star from which geometrical patterns branch out before ending up in a kind of labyrinth. Can life be like that, you asked, does it begin at a point as if it were a petal only to disperse later in all directions? What an odd question. By way of a reply I thought of taking you to look at the stars from the Ulug Beg observatory, with its immense astrolabe, maybe more than 90 feet tall, which makes it possible to determine the position of the stars and the planets by simply observing how the light diffused by an aperture in the building falls on the interior. Is it specular? I asked you. What? you replied. I was wondering if the sky is specular to the concept you were expounding about life, I said, it's not an answer, I was answering your question with another question. Then, in a market farther away you felt you were sterbing for a bukhara the color of lapis-lazuli, but it was a short-lived sterbination, we don't have enough money, you said, we'd have to skip at least two meals, and maybe in Bukhara we'll find a nicer one that costs less. And instead, just fancy that, we didn't go to Bukhara. Goodness knows why we decided not to go there, do you remember? I sincerely don't. We were tired, that's for sure, and besides that journey had been so intense, and so full of emotions and images and faces and landscapes, that we felt we were exaggerating. It's like when you go into a museum that's too big and too well-stocked and you decide to skip a few rooms to prevent more beauty being superimposed over the beauty already seen and, by surfeit, annulling the memory of the previous beauty. And besides, life was calling us back to reality, everyday life sometimes grants a few apertures, but they close up again instantly.

That aperture has reopened only now, after many years. And so I set to thinking over the things that never got done, it is a difficult but necessary thing to take stock of, sometimes it can even confer a kind of lightness, like a childish, gratuitous contentment. And for the same reason, and with the same childish, gratuitous contentment, I consequently started thinking over the books I never wrote and that I nevertheless recounted to you in exactly the same detail with which we didn't make the journey to Samarkand. The last one I didn't write, which is also the last one I recounted to you, was called *Cercando di te* and it was subtitled "A mandala." The subtitle referred to the search for the character, in the sense that his path was a concentric, spiral one, and the characters, as you know, weren't mine, I had stolen them from another novel. You know, I found it almost unbearable that that disenchanted novel full of cheerful ghosts might finish without the two characters, him and her, managing to find each other again. Was it possible that that "him," whose ostensible sarcasm concealed in reality an incurable melancholy, and that that "her," so generous and passionate, might no longer meet, almost as if the author had wanted to make fun of them and enjoy their unhappiness? And besides, I thought, in reality she had not disappeared at all, as the author wanted to have us believe, she had not exited the landscape at all; on the contrary, she was really in plain view, right in the middle of that picture, and she couldn't be seen precisely because she was too conspicuous, concealed beneath a detail, in fact concealed beneath herself, rather like Poe's purloined letter. And this is why I set him in search of his beloved, and circle after circle, as the circles got tighter and tighter, just as in the mandala, he managed to reach the center, which was also the meaning of his life, and that is to find her again. A rather romantic novel, wasn't it? Maybe too much so, but this isn't the reason why I didn't write it: in reality that novel would have been the masterpiece of all my unwritten novels, the master work of the silence I had chosen for a lifetime. A minor masterpiece, I mean to say, not one of those monumental novels that are a publisher's delight and that I have never even considered not writing for so much as a moment: in short, a little thing of no more than ten chapters, a hundred pages: a golden mean. Not writing it took me exactly four months, from May until August, and in truth I could have not written it even sooner, if I had had more free time, but my days, then, were taken up with other things altogether, unfortunately. I finished it on the tenth of August. I recall the date because the night of St. Lawrence's Day has always been a special one for us, especially for you, because of the wishes you can make looking at the shooting stars that fill the sky at that time. And then I came to visit you that very evening, you must remember, I had spent those four months in that country house, in that muggy heat that suffocates the throat and drenches the bones; you used to call me every day to ask me: Why don't you come? I've told you why not, I repeated to you, I have started not to write a complex novel that is making me sweat more blood than the infernal heat of this countryside; look, it'll be good, I assure you, or maybe strange, stranger than me, a creature as strange as some unknown beetle left fossilized in a stone, as soon as I get there I'll tell it to you.

I recounted it to you that night, on the balcony of the house by the sea, watching the shooting stars leaving white streaks in the night sky. I remember well what you said to me when I finished, but despite that I want to repeat a chapter to you. But this time I won't summarize it as I did that night, I will transcribe it for you as if I were copying it, because naturally it exists word-for-word in my memory, which imagined it. It doesn't exist in concrete form anywhere, of course. In short: where doesn't matter, provided it is nowhere. And you know how much it costs me to break this secret pact with myself and render written and visible, and hence present, words that existed only in ethereal form, light, winged and uncatchable, and free to be in not being, just like thought. And how peremptory they become here on paper, and almost vulgar, and gross, with the irremediable arrogance of the things they are. It doesn't matter, I'll do it all the same: at bottom you too loved the interstices between things, but then you opted for things in the round, and maybe you did well, because it is a form of safeguard, or in any case of acceptance of what we all are. Ah, que la vie est quotidienne!

I shall try to spare you the descriptions and the narrative passages. I didn't like them when I wrote them mentally, never mind when actually writing them down. Only the necessary information: we're in chapter eight, and in search of her he comes to a strange place in the Swiss Alps, a Zen Buddhist community, or something of the kind, because he has sensed that she has probably lost herself in this kind of research, which would now seem New Age, but many years ago (when I didn't write it) didn't smack of that at all. And in that place he dines and stays overnight, he too like a pilgrim in search of something, which is true, moreover. And over dinner he starts talking with a lady at the table. She is no longer young, a Frenchwoman, the ambience, as you will remember, is redolent of the Orient, with Indian ragas or Indian food like gosht and vegetarian meatballs, details that I spare you because I find them irritating. And at a certain point the lady says something strange: that she is there because she had lost the boundaries. And now I have to use quotation marks, and you've no idea how much I dislike that.

"Here there are rules, it's true, but rules are of use when the boundaries are lost, and besides there is also a more practical reason: at bottom this is a refuge."

"What do you mean, when the boundaries are lost? I don't understand."

"You'll understand if we continue to talk, but in the meanwhile it would be a good idea to choose dinner, with your permission I'll explain this evening's menu."

[Omissis . . . the music changed, now you heard the sound of tambourines. Omissis . . .]

"I'm sorry but I'd like to understand what losing the boundaries means."

"It means that the universe has no boundaries, and that's why I'm here, because I too have lost the boundaries."

"And that means?"

"Do you know how many stars there are in our galaxy?"

"I have no idea."

"About four hundred billion. But in the known universe there are hundreds of billions of galaxies, the universe has no boundaries."

[The woman lit an Indian cigarette, one of those scented ones, made with a single leaf of tobacco . . . Omissis]

"Many years ago I had a child, and life took him away from me. I had called him Denis, and nature had been ungenerous with him, yet he had his own form of intelligence. And I understood that."

[Omissis . . .]

"I loved him as you can love a son. Do you know how you can love a son? Much more than yourself: that's how you can love children."

[Omissis . . .]

"He had his own form of intelligence, and I studied it. For example, we had found a code, one of those codes that they don't teach in schools for children like my Denis, but one that a mother manages to invent with her own child, like tapping a glass with a spoon, dling dling, do you see what I mean?"

"Could you be more explicit, please?"

"It's necessary to study the frequency and the intensity of the message, and I know about frequency and intensity, it was part of my profession studying the stars at the astronomical observatory in Paris, but it wasn't so much this that guided me, it was because I was his mother and because we love our children more than we love ourselves."

[*Omissis* . . .]

"Our code worked perfectly, we had studied a language that humans don't know, he knew how to say I love you Mummy, I knew how to reply you mean the world to me, and other things again, everyday things, certain needs of his, but more complex things too, if I was sad, if I was happy, if he was sad, if he was happy, because even the people nature has been unkind to know like us and even more than us what happiness and unhappiness are, melancholy and good spirits, all the things that we feel and consider normal."

[*Omissis* . . .]

"But life is not only ungenerous, it is unkind too, what would you have done?

"I don't know. I really don't know. What did you do?"

"When he passed away, during the day I would wander around Paris, looking at the shop windows, the clothed beings that walked, that sat on the park benches or at the café tables, and I thought about the kind of organization we have given to life on planet Earth, I spent the nights at the observatory, but those telescopes had become insufficient. I wanted to observe the great interstellar spaces, I was like a tiny dot that wants to study the boundaries of the universe, it was the only thing that interested me, as if it might give me a little peace. What would you have done, in my place?"

[*Omissis* . . .]

"In the Andes, in Chile, there is the highest observatory in the world, and one of the best equipped too, they needed an astrophysicist, I sent off my resumé, they called me, and I left . . . "

"Go on, please."

"I asked to work with the radio telescope, to study extragalactic nebulae, do you know what the Andromeda Nebula is?

"Naturally not."

"It's a spiral system similar to the Milky Way, yet it is tilted in such a way that the arms of the spiral are not perfectly visible. Up to the first years of the last century we weren't sure if it was outside the Milky Way, it was only in 1923 that a scientist studying the Constellation of the Triangle solved the problem: those arms are the boundaries of our system, the boundaries of the universe."

[*Omissis* . . .]

"The radio telescope is used to try to pick up radiogalactic emissions with modulated signals coming from possibly intelligent creatures, and in our turn we send out modulated messages . . . "

[*Omissis* . . .]

"Oh, you cannot imagine what it means to be on one of the highest mountains in the world, while outside there is only snow and storm, as you send messages toward the Andromeda Nebula . . . and one night, one stormy night, with the ice caked on the glass of the observatory dome, an idea came to me, it was an absurd idea and I don't know why I'm telling you about it . . . "

"Please go on, really, please do."

"I told you, it was a crazy idea."

"Please."

"Well, I was sending modulated messages and that night I looked for a modulation that I had in the computer memory and then I chose a code, a code that only I knew, I translated it into mathematical modulation and I sent it . . . it's madness, I told you."

"Please."

"I don't know if you realize, but to send a message to the Andromeda Nebula, considering the light years, you need a hundred of our years, and another century before you get a reply. It's absurd, you will think that I'm a madwoman."

"No, I don't think that, I think that anything can happen in the universe, please, go on."

"The ice crystals were condensing on the glass, it was night, I was sitting in front of the telescope like someone who has committed an absurdity, and in that moment the reply from Andromeda arrived, it was a modulated message, I ran it through the decoder and I recognized it immediately, the same frequency, the same intensity: in mathematical terms it was a message that I had heard for fifteen years of my life, my Denis's message. Do I seem mad to you?"

"No, I don't think so, perhaps the universe is."

"What would you have done?"

"I don't know, frankly I couldn't tell you."

"I discovered in a sacred Indian text that the cardinal points can be infinite or nonexistent as inside a circle, a thought that disquieted me, because you can't take the cardinal points away from an astronomer. And that's why I am here, because you cannot think you can reach the boundaries of the universe, because the universe has no boundaries."

You know, my love, I wouldn't have written you all this if it weren't so late, that is to say if I weren't on the wrong side of summer, in the sunny days of December. But the pages of that novel that I didn't write reawakened in me the journey that we never made, perhaps because they talk of stars, and the sky has so many stars that it's a small loss if one or two of them fall, and we tried to understand their topography, that September 24 of many years ago, because we spent a whole night of the journey we never made to Samarkand at the Ulug

Beg observatory. What foolishness to study the stars, eh? It is the ground we should be looking at, the ground, because life always obliges us to bow our head.

Recently I have started studying a bit of Uzbek. Just for fun, the way you study certain languages in the perfect traveler's handbook, and besides, I read that studying languages at a certain age prevents Alzheimer's disease. Do you remember how funny this language seemed to us when we heard it spoken? For example "Goodbye," which also means "adieu," is a funny word because it sounds almost Spanish: *alvido*. But perhaps the funniest formula is *men olamdan ko'z yaempman*. But this is a literary expression. The simpler, more familiar form is *men ko'z o'ljapman*. Do you know what it means? It's a verb. It means "Ich sterbe," my love.

The Character Actor
is Weary

My sweet Ophelia,

The time always comes when you realize that the successive illusion of the days, or their music, has come to an end. If it was illusion, it's like when, as dawn breaks, the contours of reality, no longer blurred as before, are struck by the growing light to become nitid, sharp as a knife blade, and unremitting. If it was music, it is as if the notes of an orchestra, after the *allegro*, the *scherzoso*, the *adagio*, and the *allegro maestoso*, became solemn and slowly died away: the lights are dimmed and the concert is finished.

Today I went out of our little theater and I saw that the sky above London had unexpectedly lit up with an unusual orange light that does not belong to our sunsets, even though it would suit this weary September while the autumn equinox is in preparation. But it is a light that almost loses color; from orange it fades into violet and indigo, the way it does in certain southern cities, cities of water and marble, the light that Turner went to find in Venice. Here there is gray stone, and for water we have only this slow-running Thames, and I set to walking along its banks. I didn't go very far, I stopped near Embankment Station, and in the meantime I was thinking, letting my thoughts flow free, and all the while, like my thoughts, the Thames too was rolling along in the same direction as I was, and it seemed to me that it was telling me an old story, as old as ours, the one we were obliged to act out for years. How many years?, I asked myself. Oh, too many, if I think about it, really too many, twenty at the beginning of the year and now almost twenty-one, my sweet prince, you would answer me melancholically from your dressing room. My

Sweet Ophelia, for over twenty years you have been floating at the whim of the current, for twenty years I have watched you drown, and I know I am the cause of your death.

I was looking at the slow current of the river and I was thinking of the years gone by, of the fires of enthusiasm, of the steady settling down into a kind of habit that becomes a refuge, after which the slow illusion of the days becomes the slow illusion that tomorrow might be different from today. No: tomorrow cannot be different, little Ophelia, tomorrow I shall still tell you incoherent things, I love you, I love you not, I am chasing the rats out of my palace, I shall mock your brother and run your father through, that fool Yorick will stand motionless before me his arm outstretched to show me a pumpkin and you with your heart broken will abandon yourself to the whim of the current. And in that moment, as the lights fade to azure, the actors will stand stock-still on the stage to create that expectant pause that must capture the audience, the music from the loudspeakers will sing *Yesterday, all my troubles seemed so far away*. And as always we will rely on the music of the Beatles to renew a tragedy centuries old.

But our soundtrack was impressive, back then, wasn't it, little Ophelia? How new it was, how well it went down with the audience, the press, the public, because in a little theater in Soho a company of young students had renewed the eternal tragedy dressed in drainpipe pants and playing Beatles music. I would arrive in my Mini, and, getting out in front of the fans, walking around the car and opening the door for you as if you were a noblewoman truly worthy of Prince Hamlet, I would usher you out with a majestic bow, doffing my plumed hat with a flamboyant gesture. Oh, distant Ophelia, it was the end of the sixties, we felt young and we were young, London seemed like a party, and life too. Perhaps our most brilliant stunt was to use to big eighteenth-century marionettes for Rosencrantz and Guildenstern. Two mechanical puppets constructed by craftsmen of that epoch who aimed to produce automatons similar in every way to human beings, two puppets that moved sad faces on which we had placed two Pierrot-style tears, while two voices from the wings recited their parts to produce an extraordinarily disturbing effect. Look, dear spectators, these are the real actors, they are mechanical marionettes with tape recorders inside their wooden bellies, they have no innards, they have no heart, they have no soul, all they have is wood shavings and a magnetic tape that feigns their emotions. Make your theater for me, I tell them. Rosencrantz kneels down and his metallic joints creak sinisterly in the auditorium. Guildenstern has taken up a pitiable pose, like someone with a bellyache. He has a letter in his hand, and he proffers it to Rosencrantz, who is holding a letter out to the king of a distant land. Sire, says Rosencrantz, with this letter we must betray the Prince of Denmark, I pray you accept it for this is the wish of my accomplice Guildenstern. Sire, says Guildenstern, with this letter we must betray the Prince of Denmark, I pray you accept it for this is the wish of my accomplice Rosencrantz. Sire, say Rosencrantz and Guildenstern in unison, as a token of our betrayal please accept our Pierrot-style tears. I leap to my feet, all this strikes me as intolerable, these two stupid wooden dummies are working on my emotions, trying to shock me, to touch my weakest and most craven part, they are blackmailing me, do they perhaps think they can catch me in their trap? Ah!, it's not so easy with the bold Prince of Denmark. He unsheathes his small-sword, he points it at them, he challenges them, threatens them. Villains, two-bit hams, you who are not even hams because you are mechanical creatures, did you think to move the vasty spirit of a courageous prince? One of their heads, rotated by an internal mechanism, has turned to one side so that the public can clearly see the Pierrot-style tear that furrows its cheek, and the lighting engineer's spotlight, like a knife point, pierces that tear, the crystal of a trinket that once served as a common woman's earring that we bought at the flea market to stick on the cheek of this fake actor. And how it glitters, that tear, falser than any other false thing, so that the public might weep real tears, in exchange for the illusion we sell every evening for the price of a ticket. But the Prince of Denmark will not permit the public to weep for an actor that is not he: he brings his small-sword up to the throat of the companion of that dissembler who is pretending to weep, and he asks him: Does he weep? What's Hecuba to him? Distraught, truly distraught is that young prince whom specters grant no rest, and tormented are his nights, for he knows that the nefarious queen lies with her lover, mocking the memory of his father. He holds his head between his hands, he turns to the moon, he is assailed by the most dismal melancholy, his soul is black with soot. Poor deluded little Ophelia, do you think you can assuage his suffering with your ingenuous words of love?

And so the years go by, and we get older, stuck with the mask that has been imposed upon us, even though we chose it ourselves. The articles in the papers get rarer, until one day the press ignores you. The youthful, enthusiastic public that once sat before you now brings kids along with them: they are their children, who can already see with historical hindsight how an avant-garde company of the sixties interpreted Shakespeare in the sixties, now that we are nearing the end of the century. And in this way your death too may become part of a historical process, my little Ophelia, your suicide for an eccentric prince, your inconsolable desperation, your floating in a plastic pond wearing a Mary Quant miniskirt.

Without realizing it I had come to Russell Square; then I went into Covent Garden and bought a ticket for the Theatre Museum. So I set to wandering around the rooms, finally like he who looks on, and is not looked at. And I lingered in the rooms where some models illustrate the evolution of theater houses from Shakespeare's time up to the present day, and then the rooms where the posters are hung, along with the programs and costumes of the most celebrated shows that we staged for over twenty years. And for me it was a surprise tinged with distress to see how everything grows old in the theater except the spirit of the theater itself. The old, unchanging tragedy of the bizarre Prince of Denmark and his unhappy beloved remained identical in every period, and yet how ugly and dated were the faces and costumes of the actors, and the stage sets. It was all old, and out of fashion, because even in the attempt to copy the antique every epoch left itself and the time it brought with it indelibly impressed on the clothes and the faces of the actors. And I thought that soon we would be there too, among those posters and those costumes: I with my hair down to the nape of my neck, like the Beatles, hair that is getting thinner now, and you, poor Ophelia, whom I forced to commit suicide in a miniskirt every evening. And really I was seized by a shudder, and a kind of madness: the rooms were deserted, I chose one where a famous actress of the thirties gazed at me with a tragic and opaque look from a yellowing poster. And then I don't know what came over me, I knelt down before her, I said to her: Pray, love, remember, and I spoke to her of love-in-idleness and I told her that the tongue speaks with strange notes, it darts like that of a serpent, it slips sideways, and then I told her: Get thee to a nunnery: why wouldst thou be a breeder of sinners? I am myself indifferent honest; but yet I could accuse me of such things that it were better my mother had not borne me: I am very proud, revengeful, ambitious, with more offences at my beck than I have thoughts to put them in, imagination to give them shape, or time to act them in. What should such fellows as I do crawling between earth and heaven? And I embraced the air before me as if that essence of Ophelia I was addressing were really you, and it seemed to me that for the first time in our life I had managed to express my love for you, my eternal incommensurable love that is nevertheless sick, because the Prince is sick, dear sweet Ophelia, he is gnawed by an unknown disease that is draining his soul and at the same time filling his body with bilious and malign humors, oh, who is this man I have been for so many years and still do not know?, who is this creature tormented by doubts and insomnia who is on the lookout for ghosts and believes in Eternity? And why did that dull-witted and contorted being let you, kind Ophelia, drown every evening in a plastic tub wearing a white Mary Quant miniskirt? Could I not, perhaps, have said a little more to you? Was the script that I had to follow so binding and immutable?

No, it wasn't. I threw myself at your feet and finally before the yellowing photograph of that old actress I spoke words I was never able to say to you in all these years. They are poor words, because I am not that great playwright who imprisoned us, making us what we are, mine was a poor childhood redolent of poverty and the wrong side of the tracks, I am only a poor actor, and my accents are limited. But I said to you: Sweet Ophelia, you know, I didn't want to hurt you the way I did. With you, I would have liked to be honest and normal, a taxpayer, like all the men who come back home and pay their taxes, and who know that their pension is due them because they have done an honest job all their lives; they have filed away the dossiers on other people's taxes, they have stamped papers in some state office, they have punched the tickets of the passengers on the trains that run through our country. And I made you a poem, forgive the poor verses, extrapolated the way one does when the memory functions in fits and starts:

O cosmetics of the heavens,
Heal my beloved!
She has sea-green eyes,
And weeps for my blackness.
I wear a black cloak,
And black is my soul, they say, but I love you,
*   sweet Ophelia,*
I have an immaculate soul,
Whiter than your miniskirt.

And like the men I was talking to you about, the honest men who arrive at their deserved pension, O my sweet Ophelia, you who have put up with my tedious presence for a lifetime, I would like it if you said to me: Richard, our grandson has arrived, he's in his bedroom, now I'm going to call him so that you can play with him. And even though we don't have a grandson because we never had children and you committed suicide before that could happen, you will go gracefully to the guest room in an honest dressing gown and slippers lined with mock velvet, not in a Mary Quant miniskirt, and you will come back to the living room holding a little boy by the hand, saying, Francis, say good evening to grandfather, who has come home from work and will play with you now. Ah, but I knew that little Francis was going to be our guest this weekend, I'm hardly as naïve as you think, my little Ophelia, and why don't you both just take a look at the surprise that grandfather has brought with him? And so I open the parcel I was nonchalantly carrying under my arm and I take out a train set that will delight little Francis. It has all the trimmings, mountains and tunnels that the engine must pass through, a little lake made of silver paper, two grade crossings and a village that is absolutely identical to the one we live in, because it's nice to live in the country at our age, isn't it? Ophelia, you know, when you asked me to leave

London I was a bit reluctant, I thought that I would become melancholy living among grassy meadows and flocks of sheep, with the village pub as the only distraction. And what a joy for little Francis who has been wishing for a toy like this since last year. Too expensive, you told me last Christmas, but now, sorry, I have really done the craziest thing, you know, the retirement bonus on my pension has allowed me to indulge in a little financial folly that will be the joy of a delightful grandson like ours, and how glad I am to see that finally you agree about this too, in fact, you are happy, and how it bucks you up to get down to playing with your grandson right away, you have wanted to do this for some time, haven't you? But your sense of economy did not allow you to, and so all three of us are fascinated, you and I as well, like two children, as we watch the mechanical train going around and around through mountains, valleys and villages, while at the press of a button the grade crossing closes so that it may proceed on its triumphal way.

And in that moment a custodian appeared at the door and eyed me in amazement. What are you doing?, he asked me in inquisitorial tones. I am reciting Hamlet's soliloquy to Ophelia, kind sir, I replied. This isn't the place for speechifying, was the custodian's surly reply, you can do that in Hyde Park, where everyone can say what he wants. And how could I explain to him that that was Hamlet's soliloquy, *my* soliloquy, the one I should have really delivered to you, sweet Ophelia, instead of murmuring those incoherent words that led you to commit suicide every evening.

I went out into the open and night had fallen. The lights of London, few and far between, shone in the park. Behind them you could glimpse the buildings of the city, life. I learned only yesterday that you are leaving our little company. You are the best actress of all of us, or at least, whereas we are completely forgotten, you are the one that the press still remembers. But I don't think that this is the reason why you decided to take a part in another drama. It's not because you're a good actress, it's because you're tired: tired of my incoherent words, tired of dying every evening. And maybe you also want to love, in a way that I was never able to love you. You know the risks that the new life will involve for you, but you prefer them to my inconclusive madness. You will be seduced by Don Juan, because being seduced is your role, and seducing you is his. But at least, for the time that remains to you, what a novelty, what a shot in the arm! I don't like Don Juan, and I wouldn't make a good actor for that part. Whereas it may not seem so, he is more tragic than I am, even though he is so well mannered, apparently carefree, courteous, and with a keen sense of the civility of conventions; he is much madder than I am, because he is banal, indeed, perhaps he is an old idiot who sees the world as if it were a woman, and would like to copulate with it. He is semi-impotent, and cannot become aroused unless he practices his wretched arts of seduction. I shall leave him to practice them on you, and let him play his part, as the script demands, because I could never be him. But I don't want to lose you, little Ophelia, I cannot, and that's why I too have left the company and I have asked for a part in this new production that is competing with us. I have specified that I will accept any part, even the paltriest, even the most insignificant, even in drag, as long as I may be on the same stage on which you are performing. I could say to you as if you were Mathurine: let her believe what she will. Or as if you were Carlotta: let her dream on. Or, as if you were once more Mathurine: all other countenances are ugly, compared to yours. Or as if you were once more Carlotta: one cannot tolerate other women, after one has known a woman like you. No, this is no good, this is good for your Don Juan who has made you his in the house of Count Uguccio della Faggiola and in his bed, the bed of an irresistible lover. This part is not for me, I cannot be your seducer, my part is rather that of a spectator, but not of one sitting on a seat in the stalls, rather that of one who looks at you with his face petrified by time and the tedium of having tormented you for so many years. And I will say, but very softly indeed, in a sweet voice: He who dines on heavenly food needs not the food of mortals! Other more serious considerations have brought me here!

No, none of this, I will be the Ghost, the veiled woman who plays the Statue, and with a grave voice of deepest censure, I will say: Don Juan has but a moment to benefit from heavenly mercy, and should he not repent immediately, he is doomed to perdition. And then your Don Juan, that conceited windbag, will reply: who dares utter these words? I seem to recognize this voice. Sir, it is a ghost, that dupe Sganarello will chime in, I recognize it by its step, Sir. And then your Don Juan, more of a blusterer than ever, will cry out: Specter, phantasm or devil, I want to see who it is! And behold, my sweet Ophelia become Elvira become Carlotta become Mathurine, your Hamlet, finally become the ghost on whose account he tormented himself for a lifetime, will be able to play his true part, and as the script requires he will lift up the black veil that envelops his body to play Time with no escape and no remedy, death whose scythe reaps the life of men. And your Don Juan will blanch with terror, I will not be holding a scythe, however, but the feather of Hamlet's cap, and with that, as if I were writing in the air, I will start to sing: "*Querida, não quero despedida, eu fui feito pra Você, foi tão bom te conhecer na vida, não tem outra saida*, dear Ophelia, I cannot bid you farewell, I was made for you, it was so sweet having you in my life, it's a dead-end street," which is the song *Feito pra Você* by Grupo Raça, which I am learning by heart, you know, I've started studying Brazilian; it's really a fantastic language, and so much more loving than ours; had

162

Shakespeare been Brazilian he would never have made me say the words I have had to say to you all my life, and besides Grupo Raça has samba singers of all colors, just like all Brazilians; I think it's more modern than the Beatles, who by now have had their day and ours, and from behind the wings you will reply: "*Foi un rio que passou na minha vida*, it was a river that ran through my life," which given the end I always had you make produces a certain effect, and at that point Don Juan will become stiff as a corpse, there won't even be any need of the Commandant to hurl him into the inferno that he deserves, that aging suburban Don Juan, for it will be he who turns to stone, nay, to salt, like a statue of salt, and you my sweet Ophelia, finally dressed as Ophelia, will come on stage and cry to me: my sweet prince, I didn't really commit suicide at all, I merely went to get a breath of fresh air at the lake, a stroll of an evening does me good, it restores a sense of reality, but what 'a joy it is to find you in good spirits. And as the samba music swells in intensity, we will embrace each other in the center of the stage as the curtain slowly comes down, you will see how the public will be filled with enthusiasm, how they will go into raptures, they will begin to applaud and stamp their feet as they did in 1968, when we staged the first performances, won't they, little Ophelia?

Strange Way to Live

Erkennst du mich, Luft, du, voll noch einst meininger Orte? *

(RAINER M. RILKE, *Sonnets to Orpheus*)

---

* Do you recognize me, air, you so full of my former places?

My love,

A strange way to live, this, in which one night we chance to
wake up in the dark as a cock crows, and it seems as if we
are on the farm where we spent our childhood. We stare at
the darkness with eyes wide open and wait for day, and
meanwhile your childhood is there, present, beside your bed;
you could almost take it by the hand, go on, take your childhood by the hand, you tell yourself, come on, screw up your
courage, even though a long time has gone by, even though
life seems to have buried it, it's there, only a few inches away,
you have childhood at your disposal, come on, take it by the
hand, come on. Stretch out your hand in the dark and you'll
feel your childhood. It takes the form of a little girl, a little
girl with whom you are passing through your childhood
hand in hand. Ah, but that is not the childhood you had in
Barcelona, spent in a bourgeois home full of antique furniture and pictures of nationalist forebears—respectable people, however—bankers, wealthy men with those ever so virile whiskers, as virile as they had to be in order to be good
citizens who think about their wives, families, native land,
money, and even a little bit about their mistresses, because
mistresses come after everything else, like servants; no, it's
not this childhood, off with you, you childhood that passes
yourself off as true only because you're my childhood as
recorded by the registry office; you know, there's more to life
than the registry office, life is always elsewhere, the real childhood is the one you choose as an adult, or in old age, and so
take your childhood that isn't true but is nonetheless the
truest, and it is a little girl wearing wooden clogs capering on

the sand; before you there is an immensity of blue sea, and it's summer, and the little girl cuts capers and says: This is what puppets do, and then goes tralalee tralala, because we're playing a game, do you want to play with me, Enrique?, let's play ring a ring o' roses together. Oh, says Enrique the little boy who has taken too much sun and so they've smeared his reddened cheeks with a thick layer of cream: do you come from the Colón neighborhood? Stupid, Enrique, very stupid indeed, the world is not only Colón, who discovered the New World, the world is the world, it contains a neighborhood called Colón, but also a piazza Ciro Menotti, a boulevard Jourdan, and a Clot Fair, but especially, look here foolish little Enrico, it also contains this *granja*, a fine old farmhouse, or even a hotel, or whatever you want to call it, our parents have gone to the club to take tea and play canasta; they will spend the afternoon in that stupid cabin on the farm, and maybe our daddies will play pool too, a game that imitates life because it's full of right, obtuse, and acute angles, which is the path the balls must follow, but we'll go round in circles instead, ring a ring o' roses thumbs its nose at the angles, doesn't it little Enrique? Yes, yes, it's true, you whisper in the darkness to your childhood playmate, who you would like to become your schoolmate too, your bedmate, your life companion, and who will probably never be that, but now this doesn't matter a bit to little Enrique, now he is happy, he has given his hand to his real childhood, and together they play ring a ring o' roses on the half orange, which is a semicircle paved with porphyry on that immensely long esplanade that slowly advances toward the beach; it is also set a bit higher than the rest of the esplanade, and from there you can see the sea better than from any other place. And today we won't go to the beach because a southwester is blowing, and it will blow for three days. It is a warm wind that causes storms at sea and makes people irritable, but Enrique and his childhood are not irritable, they are playing ring a ring o' roses and singing a little ditty.

Na ausência e na distância, sings a voice on the street, and immediately after comes the cry: laranjas, laranjas! It is necessary to shift from childhood to the categories of the present, dawn is peeping in at the window, and a street vendor has learned a song by Cesária Évora: Africa, which Portugal conquered with arms and ships before bringing it the civilization of Christ, the tongue of the West, and slavery, now returns like a nemesis, it returns with the colorful creole that a woman selling oranges from Oporto has learned perhaps without knowing that Africa is reflected in her, and she sings softly: mansinho, lua cheia, and tries to imitate Cesária's pronunciation, but she is not barefoot like Cesária, she is wearing rubber galoshes that prevent her from slipping on the damp sidewalk of this winter day on the Oporto Riviera. She sings Africa. Africa, ah, Africa that I have never known, Africa the mother, Africa the womb, Africa that my Europe has raped for centuries, Africa the immense, poor, sick yet still cheerful despite the canker that gnaws at you, Africa that you call nha desventura, nha crecheu as they call love in your tongue, which we have mongrelized and in which a working class woman from Oporto is singing, crecheu, crecheu, crecheu, nha desventura. Africa whom damned bandits are still raping, Africa where the moon is huge and reddish as we read in exotic books, in the absence and the distance that separates me from you, Africa where many continue to write out of servility in the language in which I write for freedom, more purist than the purists, as if the shantytowns of Luanda, the lands mined by the murderers were their Royal Academy, their Port Royal, oh Africa of the wanderer Kapuscinski, of the magnificent Luandino, oh Africa that is now passing beneath the windows of this little boarding house on the Oporto Riviera through the uncertain imitation of an orange seller, Africa, please take me back home; to the home I desire, if I still have a home; well, now it is broad daylight, the winter sun casts a ray of light over the crumpled blanket at the foot of the bed, it's time to get up, it's time to go out, it's time you thought of who you are not, that's what you say to yourself in silence, it's really time you thought of who you are not.

My dear, this is what I was thinking of as I was getting dressed again, now the winter light coming from the estuary is dazzling and has become violently so in the room with its reproduction of the poor Fatima shepherds whom the naïve painter has portrayed with the expression of retarded people who deserve the Kingdom of Heaven, like all retarded people, according to Christ's alarming statement. You get dressed again and you know that it's time to end your journey, the purpose of which was unknown to you and which instead, with a clarity more dazzling than the light of day, you are aware that you know, you possess, you have made your own, and you would like it if this certainty were accompanied by Mozart's concerto for piano and orchestra in C major, for you can hear the music of it, but you want the allegro vivace with the Serkin cadence executed by the magical fingers of Maria João Pires, and you want the allegro vivace because, come on, Enrique, your journey has become an allegro vivace from the moment—yesterday evening, before you fell asleep—you read the mysterious book you chanced to find in the drawer of the bedside table. And that book by an author who had already foreseen everything about you, your itinerary, your path, made you think that maybe you were pursuing your future and at the same time it made you reacquire the meaning of what you had lost: it is your vertical journey; in its veritable, implacable and unwitting end, on the contrary, it is as if your journey had shifted to the horizontal: it's true!, it's true, you are in movement, and time passes through you, your future is looking for you, it finds you, it is living you: it has already lived you.

Finding a book that tells of your life in a drawer in a boarding house in an unknown city will strike you as a literary cliché, won't it, my love? You could say to me, what is this you are writing me here? I could reply: who is writing me? Right: who is writing me, and what am I talking to you about, at the end of the day? I am talking to you about what happened, of what my re-future wants me to be, of the reverse, complementary and necessary path dictated by a book found by chance in a drawer in a boarding house in Oporto, a city unknown to me until yesterday evening, when I moved into the room in this boarding house (a room with yellowed wallpaper in the back of the building) and I understood without any shadow of doubt that I was making my way backward along the route that an unknown writer had decided for me. Mar azul, assim mansinho, I read that book, my dear, and it talked of my route: a vertical dive into a calm blue sea, which engulfed me in its blue calm. That book had taken my memories, as if it knew them better than I, the memories of my youth, the memories of when I gathered poppies at the side of a road surrounded by wheat fields, memories of books read, of people known, even of a trip I made to an archipelago that perhaps doesn't exist any more, lost in my dreams and prey to forgetfulness, when the moon is the most dearly beloved and on the horizon all the mountains are serene, when you are yet to be remembered, not so much by those you have charmed today, but by those you still have to meet, because it is my yesterday, and I've already passed through here; that book knew this, it had already written about the time I had to pass through. And it said: "I remember that on my journey to the Azores I went into Peter's Bar in Horta, a café frequented by whalers, near the yacht club: a cross between a tavern, a meeting place, an information agency, and a post office. Peter's ended up becoming the recipient of precarious and adventurous messages that would not otherwise have had any other address to try. From the wooden notice board on the wall of Peter's Bar hang appeals, telegrams, and letters waiting for someone to come and claim them. On this board I found a mysterious succession of notes, messages, and voices that seemed to have a close relationship with one another, as if they were traveling in an imaginary caravan of invented memories, voices brought there by something, but it's impossible to say what."

That book knew everything, really, even that I was going to plunge in a free fall into the nothingness of nothing. But it didn't know that it wasn't going to be an outward journey, but an inward one. O mar, mar azul, sings the orange seller, mar piquinino, and so I went down to the street, my love, by now the broad daylight and the winter sun evoked a distant summer, and I had to remind myself who it was that liked you yesterday as if he were yet to like you, and I wondered about the reason for this journey of mine that that mysterious book hidden in a drawer of my room described in only one direction. And why therefore did the ghost of Don Juan (or James Stewart, if you will) have to like you, and why did you allow that old fool perfumed with cologne to like you, and why did that perverted will o' the wisp Leporello have to like you, and why did you allow that pervert to like you? Anyway, I bought some oranges and I ate them going toward the sea, o mar, mar azul, mar piquinino, I walked though the alleys of the Riviera, choosing the streets at random, because streets are an ideal place for the randomness life offers, looking at the boats floating in the slow current of the river.

Finally I arrived at the estuary, where I found myself facing the beach. I started pissing into the sea, taking advantage of the wind at my back. A gentleman passed by dressed like an academic, wearing a tricorne. At first I thought he looked like Marinetti; he shot me a look that I thought was of disapproval, and I said to him: Don't be scandalized, Professor, I'm adding a drop of water to the ocean, why don't you piss into the sea too? It'll do you good, you'll see, and take care not to do it on your shoes, because that can happen to academics. Great sea, the sea is truly immense, my love, mar azul, but the lua cheia hadn't risen yet, there was a violet streak on the horizon that was turning orange, maybe a storm was brewing, I really understood that I was making my way backward along the route that the mysterious book had mapped out for me, there were sails on the sea, and that made it really tiny, I went back toward town, walking slowly. I made my way back along that narrow suburban street, looking for rua Ferreira Borges, but no one seemed to know it, and at a certain point I had the impression that my uncle Federico Mayol was crossing a square beneath the fine drizzle that had begun to fall. I looked for the post office and I sent off the telegram it was necessary to send off to your Commendatore and your Leporello. My most sincere condolences, I wrote them both, I am sure that you will both miss her very much. And in that moment I understood that I really could return home, I could even leave my baggage in the boarding house, there was nothing in it, apart from four shirts and two books that I have read over and over: one is about the ghosts that a Mexican writer encountered in a night of dreams, the ghosts of señor Páramo, the other is the Gospel according to that optimist John, whom I have loved so dearly and who believed so much in the word, for in the beginning was the word and the word was life and life was the light of men. And I set off on foot toward home, toward my home. Catalonia is not that far away, after all, you can even get there on foot. But you, my love, will you be there once more? Like me, will you have made your inward journey and will everything be on the point of beginning again, starting from scratch?

The Eve of the Ascension

My sweet suffering girl,

I made you suffer, by leaving you. But I am not to blame, you know, even though there's no sense in talking about blame, and besides you could never stand the word "blame." It's true, it's an unbearable word. Let's say it was because of the Leghorn chickens, let's continue to call them that in our old code, because a transplant is no joke, we know that, what with all the other stuff lying about around that charming little thing there. But let's not talk about that anymore, okay?

Listen, even last night, which was the most beautiful night I have spent in all these years, the sweetest, the clearest, the longest, as I held you once more in my arms. I thought: I mustn't think about it anymore, we mustn't think about it anymore, that's the way it went, life's like that.

And in the meantime I heard the tolling of the bells of that village, the one immersed in olive trees that you can just see from the window of the little hotel where we wound up after having roamed the countryside all afternoon long. First, the Talking Cricket Inn. We said to ourselves: not on your life, we've had a bellyful of Talking Crickets in our life. Do you remember Rino, for example? You know that Rino came to mind, yesterday night? Yeah, Rino the revenant who suddenly popped up after an eternity. When was it, do you remember? Sixty-seven, sixty-eight? Well, something like that: Rino, the wise guy, the one who used to say that while the world is paradoxical nothing is more paradoxical than life that weds death. If I recall aright you didn't dislike him, he struck you as an interesting man, he wrote highly abstruse essays for a university meta-magazine that nobody read. "The vision makes the ecstasy more serene," he liked to say, quoting Edgar Allan Poe out of place. According to me he was shooting up, in those days everyone was shooting up, and those who weren't shooting up with needles were shooting others with handguns; shooting one to educate a hundred, if I can put it like that. Then it emerged that there was really no way the meta-magazine was a university thing, it merely served as a cover for a group of hotheads and was apparently financed by Imelda Marcos, go figure, the one who collected shoes for herself and hempen neckties for her fellow citizens. In fact, you even flirted a bit with that wise guy Rino, an intellectual wiseacre if nothing else, given that when they took him into preventive custody, the way they do around here, you kept up a close correspondence with him stuffed with Nietzsche and Shakespeare, no lightweights. But goodness knows why I am talking to you about these things, it's because last night, really, I thought about how many talking crickets we have had to put up with until we got to the age we are. But now, finally, enough.

I heard crickets, last night, but they made a completely different sound. They are the crickets heralding the coming of summer, which I think I will spend with you. The crickets of the cricket parties we held when we were kids, the ones that died on a lettuce leaf during the night in the little cage in the kitchen, even though these ones were free crickets, happy crickets, you sensed this by the way they were singing, it seemed as if they were saying "Tomorrow is the first of June, the feast of the Ascension." But what feast is that anyway, the feast of the Ascension, where do you ascend and who does the ascending? In my home there were no Catholic feast days, as you know, but perhaps they were observed in your house, because I remember the photograph of your wedding in which you are wearing a white dress, you have a veil on your head and you are kneeling before a priest. But, even though we were of another faith, as kids we loved the feast of the Ascension, because in the village they would make sweet fried pastries dusted with powdered sugar, and a neighbor lady would bring some for me and my brother; Ferruccio and I really adored them, and our mother would hide them, sharing the secret only with us, otherwise our father would have thrown them away protesting that the woman wanted to convert us.

I've lost the thread, as usual. It's probably because it's hard for me to continue, but given that I'm digressing, and given that I was talking to you about Rino, I want to tell you (but maybe you know already) that he has become a big shot in a powerful publishing house whose owner is one of those we used to call the "bosses" in the old days. Rino was up for everything, he is a real man for all seasons. Now he finally hears His Master's Voice, and maybe he has attained the peace of the senses. What a memory some people have: last month he wrote me a letter, an elegant letter on engraved notepaper. And do you know what he remembered, with pinpoint precision, as if he had recorded it in his brain? He remembered the texts that I read to you all that evening after the conference held by the old anarchist professor, and we all ended up at Rino's place, and I had my notes under my arm and I read them to you, do you remember? They were notes on those artists who had taken drugs, a rough draft of a book I had titled *The Artificial Imagination*, do you remember? Well, the really extraordinary thing was that in his letter Rino specified in minute detail those writers he did *not* want. "I'm not interested in Coleridge or De Quincy," he said, "besides, everybody knows they were addicted to opium; nor do I want Gautier, Baudelaire, Rimbaud, Artaud, or Michaux. I would especially like the pages on Savonarola who wrote *In te Domine speravi* under the influence of laudanum, because you gave a good explanation of how Savonarola made up the laudanum, mixed with rue, myrrh and honey, and the mystical effects it gave him. Then I am interested in Barbey d'Aurevilly, because you wrote that he added eau de cologne to his ether. And then I want the pages on Nietzsche, who without morphine would never have written *Zarathustra*, and Stevenson, who without morphine would never have known Mr. Hyde; and then Yeats, that mega mystic and folklorist Yeats, who together with that other blowhard Ernst Down was one of the first Europeans to try mescaline, and without that, goodbye *The Mystic Rose*. And then I want Ball, that madman with the Cabaret Voltaire, without whom Dada would have gone the same way as the dodo, he and his heroin invented in those very years; and Trakl's cocaine, Adamov's morphine, Jünger's lysergic acid, and above all Drieu, that poor diehard fascist Drieu La Rochelle, him and his syringes, his empty valise and his suicide."

This is a faithful transcription, the words are his, I have his letter in front of me. And he concludes by saying: "A little book like this, as if written by a Borges fighting for the liberalization of drugs, would be the best seller of the year." Hurray! I replied with a magical phrase: I would prefer not to.

You know, my sweet suffering girl, "I would prefer not to" has been my favorite motto over these last years. The world is full of people and everybody wants something. In my journeys to distant places I have given a lot, as you know, but almost always to people who didn't ask for anything, because they didn't expect anything from others or from the world. I recall certain paths in certain Latin American countries that led to poverty-stricken villages, and it wasn't uncommon to meet a barefoot old man, with his shirt in tatters, leaning against a hoe jammed into the barren land, and he would look at you with the serene and normal eyes of a man who has no more to say to you than Good evening: and so yes, I gave what I had, even everything, for in such moments you must give everything.

My sweet and dearest lady, in fact, my dearly beloved lady, for this is what our finding ourselves again has led to: most dearly beloved and not dearest. Most dearly beloved lady—and this is what I have tried to erase in all these years—as I write you images and words crowd my mind, the way you remain imprisoned in a dream: your shoulders, which I embrace with my arms in the half light, the words that you whisper in my ear, the way you catch me unawares in nocturnal conversation, the simultaneous, successive, and prolonged bursts of laughter, on account of your nonsense that I like so much, and even the way you squeeze the nape of my neck, gently shaking it in a gesture of false reproof (you nut!). And these images that I am describing to you, my most dearly beloved lady, are of sorrow and regret, because no one can give me back the time I let slip between the fingers of the years, no one can give us back what we lost only because I didn't have the strength not to lose it. But maybe we'll find this lost time again, my sweet love, I know we'll find it again, for it was enough for me to see that we were still young and vigorous and passionate to realize that time lost is occasionally found again, but only for the space of a few hours, those hours in which I heard you cry out for pleasure three times in a row, and then at dawn, in a drowse, as I held you tight from behind, and you took advantage of this for your pleasure and for mine.

Today I am sure that this pleasure will continue forever. My only little disappointment is that tomorrow, on this feast of the Ascension that ushers in the month of June, we will be unable to watch together the ripening ears of corn that can be seen from my window. But I understand that if you have to go pick up those documents you talked to me about you cannot be even one day late. You told me that in those papers there is an important piece of the history of this country, a country that is often devoid of history, and I think that the State

Archives, but above all the citizens, will be grateful to you for this. And so I'll expect you on the evening of June 2nd, which after all means more to me, given that it is a national holiday in honor of the Republic. And the gold of the corn will certainly be no yellower than it was yesterday. For me, it is as if time has stopped, you know?

My Light-Colored Eyes,
My Honey-Colored Hair

A good rat he was, what's more, and
One averse to all philosophical hypocrisy,
Sincere, in short, and honest too,
Albeit fed on intrigues, and fawning;
Held in popular affection, ever affable
With all, and, if one may say so, humane;
Careless of gold, but jealous of honor,
And generous, a true lover of his native land.

(GIACOMO LEOPARDI, *Paralipomeni*)

My light-colored eyes, my honey-colored hair,

You know how much and for how long I have desired you: from the first day I saw you. But then, a hundred years ago, you were a very young woman, in fact a girl in the flower of her youth. Of course, you weren't the little virgin child nor was I the dirty old man as depicted in that scandalous novel by that Russian who was an exile even from himself. But our story could begin like that just the same, because, as it is in that novel, time is fundamental to our story: a time made of nothing, just as things are also made of nothing, a "petit rien" that makes us wonder what guides things: a mere nothing, sometimes.

To tell you that I desired you from the first moment I saw you is a cliché, but that's the way it is. But then, a hundred years ago, you were in fact a very young woman, a girl in the flower of her youth ready to bloom for the one who might pluck her. I was an austere gentleman of your father's age, and the place was a vacation resort for families. And it was with families that we continued to see each other every winter, usually in February. For you, those were real vacations, for me they were barely seven days, the so-called "ski week" granted me by the provincial newspaper thanks to which I earned my living. Not a superlative salary, true, but lots of esteem, the moral and intellectual prestige of those who fought for freedom from the right side of the barricades, narrating it in a critically acclaimed chronicle that, in the eyes of all you young left-wingers from left-wing families, conferred upon me a kind of aura redolent of the romantic hero. And then, how you admired the way I used to throw myself down the slopes, tackling the most inaccessible descents, and the way I went out in foul weather. I, the fifty-year-old with the elegant and mysterious look, was more of a daredevil than you twenty-year-olds glued to the fireplace as soon as a few flakes of snow began to fall. Only you dared to keep up with me on those reckless descents: you skied like a champion, and you were afraid of nothing. I remember one morning when out of sheer defiance you followed me down the slope careless of the objections voiced by your girlfriends and your fiancé, who, terrified by the heavy snowfall, stayed in the hotel to play poker. True, the hotel, albeit apparently modest, was an extremely refined place: ten rooms, no more, fine woodwork, creaky parquet, handwoven carpets: the fact that it called itself a guest house was no more than a snobbish affectation of which we were all secretly proud. I remember that morning not ·so much because the descent was a reckless one (I had already made several followed by you) but because when you caught up with me—panting, with your cheeks ablaze, your ski jacket and the close-fitting snowsuit that outlined your long legs all covered with snow—to help yourself come to a stop you clung to the trunk of the pine tree where I was standing, and we burst out laughing like a couple of kids, not so much out of the tension released at your accomplishment of that exploit, but because you really were a kid. And we gave each other a look of complicity like two mischievous school friends. And it was with that look that everything began. I thought: This girl is mine. For it wasn't really me who was responsible for that understanding, it came from the way you looked at me. A man of that age understands how a girl looks at him, and I understood. I understood that that look contained desire, and a hint of provocation, and a tacit invitation—an offer. And I thought that, had I wanted to, I could have taken you there, right away, in the powdery snow on the edge of the woods.

Then the years began to pass. I remember you three years later, a splendid young wife with your first child in your womb, and your handsome husband, a well-mannered young man who was worried about your pregnancy and feared that, sporty as you were, you might take risks: and hence our walks together along the track packed with hard snow, all four of us, and our conversations in which my wife of that time (she was still the first, do you remember?) advised you about what kind of life to live: rest but not too much, diet, a little light gymnastics in the mornings and other trifles of that sort. Women of a certain age love to give their advice on such matters; you listened dutifully, your husband and I talked about other things.

The next time I saw you you were a young mother, holding your little kiddie by the hand and already pregnant for the second time. You were particularly exciting, you know? That winter you couldn't ski, obviously, and—very occasionally—you took a stroll as far as the village and you spent the rest of the time by the fire playing with your little boy, who was learning to walk. I remember that you kept him on his feet with a leash attached to a kind of harness around his chest and you encouraged him not to be frightened, you called him "little one" in a sweet voice. That week I dreamed more than once of possessing you, taking you from behind as I embraced your pregnant belly.

And in the meantime the winters went by, your children were getting big, our families (I mean to say your parents and I) became ever closer friends. I was getting older, my wife too, but I was as agile as ever on the slopes. I have the impression that the year I arrived with my second wife, who wasn't yet my wife, but only my "fiancée," as they used to say in refined circles in those days, you looked at me with renewed interest. Perhaps my new love had rejuvenated me, who knows. I had had my hair cropped into what was almost a crew cut, leaving a tuft at the front, and I had published a new novel that had won a prize along with laudatory reviews in certain left-wing newspapers. That evening, at dinner, it was the topic of conversation. I remember your remarks well: at that time you were still not yet the woman of letters you have become, you too frequented the world of journalism: you wrote about journeys never made and books never read for a cultural weekly. I was head over heels in love with Francesca, ça va sans dire, and you could all see that. You couldn't fail to see it. Yet an episode occurred despite this and over and beyond this, a fleeting event, which happened because it had to happen, in a natural way, like the moon rising or the snow falling. The hotel was deserted, do you remember? They had all gone to the preview of that Milanese jerk who played the painter with his left hand and the stock market with his right. I had just returned from a really long and tiring descent and on returning to the hotel I had thrown myself onto the bed and didn't wake until it was almost dinnertime and everyone had already left. But not you, you had stayed because of the children. I came down from my room and found you in front of the picture window that gave on to the valley. You had your back to me, apparently intent on looking at the lights of the village in the distance. I couldn't resist, I came up on tiptoe, I lightly touched your hair, hair the color of honey, and I said: you dreamer. Then you turned around and kissed me on the mouth. And then, with your index finer on the lips you had kissed, you whispered shhhh. Don't say a word, John, please, now is not the time, don't say anything. And I said nothing.

When he came into your life, I understood right away that the man you had been waiting for had arrived, a man with whom you were in love in a way that had never happened to you before, not with your husband, that's for sure, or with those two or three occasional lovers that had chanced to cross your path. You will be wondering how I knew. I might answer you by saying that I know women, and you know that, and that I manage to understand a certain light that comes into their eyes when they are in love, and that I can spot a dreamy smile, and a smile out of place offered to no one if not to the person they have in mind; and certain other things, which are details moreover, and details are always fundamental. What's more, I know all about the Milan of those years and the circles you frequented: the intellectual salons, the feminists, those who dreamed of the Revolution, the passwords for the street, and then back home in the evenings to listen to good music in comfort. But he did not belong to that category. And above all, he didn't write. Apparently he said that writing was something that cheapened thought, and that it was always better to talk to people, and that books, if anything, ought to be written only mentally.

And I understood that you loved him without remission one evening at dinner in the hotel, while we were eating game accompanied by bilberry sauce as prescribed by the local cuisine, and you said: I know a short story called *Quails à la Clémentine*, a friend of mine told me about it, it is the story of a story, in fact it is the story of a hypothetical theatrical piece, and it begins like this: There is a theater in Paris, in rue Sainte-Lazare, and on the stage of this theater there is a blue drawing room decorated in the Oriental manner with windows and delicate white muslin drapes, and when the drapes over the four windows are opened you can see four different shows, which are in reality different only up to a certain point, because each show talks about the same life, which is the life of a man and a woman.

And he sure couldn't have been living in Milan, a character like that whom no one knew and who thought up short stories without publishing them when everyone was desperate to get published and talked of quails *à la Clémentine* and of four windows from which you could observe four different points in the same life, like the cardinal points: one to the north, which was the past, one to the west, which in that moment Clémentine had chosen as hers, one to that east she would never have known, and the last to the south, which was her destiny and perhaps her death. A meridian death, those were your words. Do you remember? It was snowing heavily that day, perhaps the first snowfall of the year, yes, it was a New Year's Day of many years ago, how many? Nineteen, twenty; it was the beginning of the so-called magnificent eighties, and that evening we celebrated together, families and all, even your kids, who were already quite big, holding orange sodas served in champagne glasses to make a toast: Happy New Year, Happy New Year and all the best for nineteen eighty-one. Yes, it was nineteen eighty-one, I remember well, New Year's Day. And, between one toast and the next, laughing and joking, you said: I've met a guy who writes wonderful things and couldn't give a damn about getting them published; he doesn't come to Milan on principle, and he has a passion for Leghorn chickens, he's raising four of them because they lay an egg every day, shall we make a toast to him? And we toasted him. A little moron in the company, a character who was in the "protest movement" and who affected crew neck sweaters, pontificated condescendingly: Okay then, let's drink to this poor fool, hard times are in store for him. And everyone laughed, because there really was plenty to laugh about in that mountain chalet warmed by our breath and champagne toasting a poor shit who raised Leghorn chickens: we, the people of the Left, we who were "vigilant," as they used to say then, and who within two weeks would exercise our vigilance by presenting in a renowned bookstore the latest product by the crewneck intellectual, *Revolution and/or Seduction*. And I thought: that's it then, she's in love.

As you know, my light-colored eyes, my honey-colored

hair, I have a sixth sense. I've always had it, and it is what has guided me through life. I thought: Farewell my lovely, you are headed for Leghorn chickens, I'll never catch you now. But life always reserves big surprises: all you need is the patience to wait for it to offer you them. And I had no lack of patience, as you can see. The years were going by, they were going by more for me than for you. I thought of you every day, and those few days of the year I could see you in that mountain hotel, which I couldn't stand any more by then, were almost a torment. And in the meantime you were happy. Because people can be happy, in their meantimes. But yours lasted too long, really too long, believe me. In my meantime I had published other books and I recall the day in which I offered you them with that dedication: "To you, with the complicity that unites us." Once I confessed to you that, despite the books I had written and with which I courted you with knowing or futile dedications, I was not a writer. In the sense that being a writer is an ontological thing, I added, either you are or you aren't, and it's not enough to have written a few books to be a writer. And you concurred, oh yes, sure, I was really right, and you talked with the pretentiousness of a "profound" understanding of literature. Foolish girl. It was a trap: I am a *real* writer, the proof of this is this letter you are reading, and I can imagine your amazement. There is always something to understand belatedly, life deserves to be lived all the way through merely for this. But I too discovered something belatedly: that you are an illogical person, or one with a logic all her own, as when at the end of our conversation about writing, and as if it had something to do with the book I had dedicated to you with complicity, you declared: I like the tuft above your forehead. What on earth was the complicity that united us? My light-colored eyes, my honey-colored hair, you know better than I: it was simply the desire to go to bed together. Yours equal to mine, only you couldn't do it, because your head was full of the guy who raised Leghorn chickens.

Do you want to know something? I'll confess: the novel *Betrayals*, which I gave you with that dedication, was written thinking of you, and I thought of you because I had the kind of wife with whom I was "happily married" and in my boring ménage I needed to insert a really necessary and special third person, and I had sensed that you could have loved me with all of your senses, with the abandon that I desired, only if you, as you let yourself be possessed by me, were thinking of the person you loved. And only in this way would you have attained great intensity in the act of love, as great and complete as you have always dreamed. But then, apparently, you didn't understand. And, in the meantime, the years were going by. Painfully for me, and with difficulty, because a man grows old even if he stays thin, without a trace of a gut, with a tuft over his forehead and a roguish air. You know where he grows old? In his organ, forgive the crude word, and I know that you will forgive me, because though you won't tolerate crude words in public, you don't dislike them in intimacy.

But one day passes, and the next, until the day came in which your gallant Sir Anselm did not return, probably he had donned his helmet in order to avoid getting hurt too badly and had set off on one of his pointless duels, maybe with chickens of a different breed than his Leghorns. And so: and so it happened then, and that's how it was, as the poet would have put it, do you remember? There was washing hanging out to dry, still as it was in the poem. We have only to follow it, just as I followed it, even though you were the one who called me. And in fact, in the grassy yard bordered by cherry and peach trees, hanging between two branches, there was washing hung out to dry in a sea breeze that heralded September. The excuse (because it really was an excuse on your part) was that I should offer my book to the municipal library complete with a dedication from the author; they'd be proud of it, you said, it was a left-wing town, and the area had been partisan country. So much the better. On the way, we talked. I write too, you told me, in fact I have written something. What? Poems, but I'd prefer to say prose poems, stuff like that. Why don't you read me one? If you really want, but I'm a bit embarrassed, and besides I'm a lousy reader. We sat down in the deck chairs under the cherry tree, you didn't know how to begin, sometimes we feel uncomfortable, especially if we know how it's going to end, and both of us knew how it was going to end. Which one shall I read you? You choose. I could read you one in the style of Baudelaire, it's set in a little hotel in the mountains and it has the advantage of brevity. I like the idea, it reminds me of something. What's the title? It doesn't have a title, I ought to find one for it. Yes, that would be a good idea, it could become an eponymous title, books need an appropriate title. But these little poems will never become a book, you said. Of course they will, I reassured you, you know better than I, I'll see to it, read please.

When you finished reading you looked toward the horizon, and your eyes were moist. Night was falling and on the plain overlooking the sea the first lights were switched on. Why don't you call the *Leghorn chicken*, I suggested, and then I added: I'll have to find a hotel, I'm getting on in years for night driving, and besides it's a long journey. Stay and sleep with me, you said, maybe I won't wake up with a start the way I've been doing for months. I am old, I said to you. You gave a provocative smile. Oh, it's not what you are thinking, I pointed out, I'm as good as I was years ago, when I started to desire you, but you see, then . . . Then what? I mean to say, a twenty-year-old woman can go to bed with a man of fifty, but afterward . . . then it's a different thing, it's strange, that's it, maybe it's only strange, or a bit stranger.

My light-colored eyes, my honey-colored hair, the

moments of love I lived with you over these five years were sublime, even though they were rare, punctuated by intervals that seemed immensely long to me and reserved for a few privileged weekends, for encounters that we always tried to pass off as casual, and on those occasions I tasted the most sublime physical pleasures I had known in all my life. Yet, even in the moments of the greatest passion, I felt that something was missing in the quest for that total ecstasy, an ecstasy that was there, within reach, but seemed unwilling to let itself be grasped: a "petit rien" that I couldn't identify, and you couldn't either, perhaps it was the awareness that our love was too secret, and hence too free, and hence gratuitous, which deprived it of that hint of provocation or sense of sinfulness that might lend an unusual affair like ours that subterranean frisson, that spice that makes it even rarer and more febrile. This is why, after our first encounters in Milan, I began to invite you to my place in the country, taking advantage of my wife's absences: because it was the real family home, because it was there that I was happily married (but what does "happily married" mean?); in that house I lived a perfect married life, and in that bed, in that big antique bed where I made love to you, my wife and my daughter-in-law had given birth, that big bed had a long history, it had witnessed the lives of many people.

The bed. How stupid it is to think that one bed or another may confer more savor upon the love about to be consummated in it. And yet I realized this only yesterday, my honey-colored hair, and as you can see there is always something to learn in life, even at my age. For this night spent together, this sublime, clear, windless night that the Catholic calendar has chosen for one of its most beautiful feast days, was an ascension for me too, in the most earthly sense of the term, because I ascended to the seventh heaven, the one where pleasure is total and absolute. Ours was an appointment made some time before, and you have never missed an appointment. And besides, my wife was going to spend her first weekend in the mountains, and we couldn't miss a chance like that. But you were perturbed about something, I understood that from your phone call: there is something I must tell you, an important and definitive thing, I am coming only for this, only for this, do you see?—not for what you are thinking.

But no, you hadn't come only to tell me something important and definitive. You had come to love me again, or at least for one last time. I understood this as we ate dinner on the veranda. I had prepared the delicacies of which you are so fond: foie gras on a lettuce leaf, cold chicken with mayonnaise, and your favorite champagne. And you looked at me in the half light the way you have never looked at me in these five years, your eyes were moist, and the candle flame was flickering in your pupils. And I realized that there was a hint of anguish in that belated love you felt for me, which had come to an end, because the other love was greater and ours impossible. But, at the same time, the hurt you felt at hurting me made your love for me more precious and intense, and you could abandon yourself to it as if in a surge of forgetfulness and surrender. And so there was not even any need for you to tell me "the important thing" for which you had apparently come. It was enough to go to bed, to that big bed where we have loved each other so many times, and for me that sufficed, without your saying a word, to understand that he had returned. Because, after five years of love, for the first time, last night, you kissed my sex. And, as you gave me the gift you had never given me before, I was thinking about a poem of which I have a vivid recollection, a poem that says that all I had been up to now and all that had been denied me was now being freely offered, and yours was no homage offered by a slave girl huddled in the darkness, but a queen's gift that became mine, it circulated in my blood, and my time as a boy and the time I had left to live resurfaced commingled, because you kissed my sex. And then your passion exploded with an intensity it never had before—when I penetrated you it took only an instant, a tiny instant for that sound of pleasure and liberation and grandiose desperation that I had never heard issue from your mouth so loudly, and ah, finally, you too had attained your "petit rien," which is a surrogate for the absolute.

And now that this man has returned, my light-colored eyes, my honey-colored hair, now that he is yours once more and in your heart you no longer carry the shadow left by his leaving you, now you no longer bear within you that foolish sorrow that with my affection and my care I tried in vain to assuage in these years, but on the contrary now you feel sorry for him, because you know you betrayed him, and at the same time you feel sorry for me, thinking of the sorrow you will give me by leaving me, and finally, now our love can be full and absolute, despite my age, which is moreover of relatively little importance, because you don't mind old men if they can love you the way I do. And besides, I am already old no longer: I am young again. Truly, I am as young as I was thirty years ago, when I desired you in that far-off winter vacation and it was forbidden for me to make you mine.

Te voglio, te cerco, te chiammo,
te veco, te sento, te sonno [8]

8 Words from a Neapolitan song, which mean: "I want you, I seek you, I call you,
I see you, I hear you, I dream of you."

Dear,

He was arriving that evening from far away and he was tired. Tired with sleep, because he had slept for a long time. For how long? He felt like Sleeping Ugly in the woods. Woods in the sense of forest, that is, and midway on the journey there was a rock. And he hadn't been able to get around it, and that's why he had remained the Sleeping Ugly in the woods. And how ugly he was, in fact, and how ugly he felt, driving his jalopy drawn by two horses, while everyone passed him, speeding on the dark road. On several occasions he had been tempted to stop at an inn. Certain distant lights on the hillsides promised tranquil villages, a tasty dinner, and the guarantee of a bed. It was already warm for it was already May. And he said to himself: at my age, a journey like this, I'm almost of an age with Cicero when he wrote *De senectute*, and at the same time he tried to drive his two horses carefully as they pulled him too near the shoulder on the uphill stretches, and then there was that ridiculous body belt he wore under the pretext of backache, but with which in reality he tried to conceal a belly that was getting a bit too substantial. He thought: I'll turn back. And then he thought: I'll call her. He stopped in a parking area where Dutch truck drivers slept slumped against their steering wheels. There was a diner with neon lights and a phone booth, and you could eat a hot sandwich.

He decided to call her. He thought: a man of my age cannot turn up at a lady's home at this time of night, without advance warning, after having slept for so long in the woods. And so he put some coins in the phone in the diner while other Dutch truck drivers laughed loudly at their jokes, and he was relieved to find that her phone was busy. If it was busy, she was home and hadn't gone to bed yet. And so he asked the girl at the cash register, how many miles to Aleppo from here? The nearby city was not Aleppo, of course, but for him it was as perfumed as was the legendary city of Aleppo in his recollections of the Arabian Nights; but he asked the girl this question in his own language, which was wholly incomprehensible to her, and so all she understood was the word miles and she replied by spreading out three fingers of one hand. So, another three miles. He thought: I've arrived, it's worth a try. He climbed back aboard his jalopy, which now seemed like a sleigh to him, because it slipped rapidly down those hillsides, and his only worry was that of being Sleeping Ugly with a bit of a potbelly, because even though she was no longer young (albeit far younger than he) she had probably found a friend without a trace of a belly, one of those who don't fall asleep in the woods because they play tennis. And this gave him a twinge in his liver, which was not in perfect condition. He wondered: when Ivan Ilich began to feel a pain in his side, was it the left or the right side? Be that as it may, how much he had changed since his long sleep in the woods, not so much physically, as in his way of being. He understood this by the language he was mentally using as he drove his sleigh downhill watching himself being overtaken by reckless drivers who drove their vehicles careless of danger and their fellow man. Never, before, would he have muttered those vulgar words at them, words that were maybe even coarser than those used in Dutch by the Dutch truck drivers. And when he thought of her, in the past, or if he thought of making love with her, or of her sex, his mind, even when spurred by unrestrained passion, as it had been, would never have dared to formulate expressions in language as crude as that which he was now using in his head. For elegance of the spirit had been there to overcome the excesses of the flesh, and that decidedly brutish way of being that men sometimes adopt could be tamed by a subtle romanticism that conceals, corrects, and refines. For example, on seeing her roaming around the house in her robe, as he imagined her now, he would have said to her, quoting the French poet: In your green robe you remind me of Melusina, you walk with little steps as if you were dancing. That's what he would have said to her once upon a time. But now instead he would have said (or so he thought he would have said): You have a marvelous ass, it's one big smile, it's never tragic.

But was this any way to present himself? And what if she had a man in the house? She could very well have had a man in the house, her man. And what, for example, if at the door she were to say to him: please, lower your voice, there's someone sleeping in there. Or even worse: I would be grateful if you didn't talk so loudly, sir, Alfredo is sleeping in there. Because she could have easily fallen back on formality, after so many years of sleep, and in there there could be an Alfredo, in life at times there are men called Alfredo asleep in the next room, and who are there expressly to love, love me Alfredo.

He took an avenue full of lights. Aleppo, city of my dreams, he thought, you welcome me glittering with light, as if I were Caesar in triumph. He rolled down the window and let in the fresh night air. It bore the scent of linden trees, and maybe vanilla, the way Aleppo should smell. Perhaps it was that little cookie factory you could see on the left with a large illuminated sign: Biscou-Biscuit. Nice, what a nice name, Biscou-Biscuit. For example he could have gone about things this way: by knocking at the door, instead of ringing the bell; it was classier, a bell ringing at that time of night would make anybody jump; she would open and he would say: Hi, Biscou-Biscuit. The yellow traffic light at the bottom of the avenue began to flash intermittently, traffic signals usually do that after midnight, so it was already midnight. What would you do with someone who fell asleep in the woods for goodness knows how long, he wondered, and who shows up at your place after midnight calling you Biscou-Biscuit? I'd slam the door in his face, he replied to himself, maybe accompanied by a choice little oath or two, but delivered in a low voice, politely. Biscou-Biscuit, that's all we needed! Suddenly, at the end of the avenue crossed by the anonymous blocks, he spotted some plane trees. And suddenly, as if in a photograph, he saw again the precise geometry of that seaside city he knew so well and thought he had forgotten. There, the avenue ended at the seafront where ancient salt cedars bordered a pebbly beach; farther on there was the little harbor beyond which the historic center began, a maze of paved streets, once a fishing village. And in the middle of those tangles of alleyways a little square opened up with a white church flanked by two palm trees, the church of the two palms, and beside the church there was a portico beneath which the fishermen used to sit mending their nets on tiny blue stools that seemed made for children, and above the porticoes there were some old houses, and the one on the left, the one with the wrought iron balcony, was hers. And by now she had gone to bed, he was convinced of this, she had certainly gone to bed. Twenty minutes before the phone had been busy, therefore she was awake, but at a quarter past midnight what should a woman alone stay up for?, she goes to bed. And if there is an Alfredo, all the more reason.

The historic center had been closed to traffic, but at that hour he certainly wasn't going to encounter a traffic cop, the coast still wasn't in season. He parked beneath one of the palms, in a space reserved for handicapped drivers, because, logically, access to the center was not prohibited for them. This is just the slot for me, he thought, just what the doctor ordered. What a remote expression, just what the doctor ordered—where had that sprung from?—maybe from his adolescence, when the kids talked like that: it's just what the doctor ordered, sure as death and taxes. The balcony window was unlighted. Blasted window, blasted window, why are you unlighted? Goddamned window, goddamned window, why are you unlighted? Come on, pretty little window, come on, be nice, light up again, she's only gone to her room for a moment and she's switched off the light, but now she's coming back; light up again, she's left her glasses in the living room, she always reads before going to sleep, but without her glasses she can't see things close up, she was always farsighted, even when she was young, and if she doesn't read her two or three pages she can't get to sleep, I know better than you, light up again, don't be silly.

He sat down on the stone bench in front of the church. To ring or not to ring, that is the question. Or better: to go up or not to go up, because the little street door was open, as it always was for that matter, it gave access to three apartments, and no one bothered to close it. He thought about lighting a cigarette, just to think things over. But if you light up a cigarette, you're done for, my dear fellow, because it's the last chance, and she really has fallen asleep. At the end of the day she left her glasses on the bedside table and how many pages does it take to smoke a cigarette? Not more than two or three, and after two or three she falls asleep with her book on her breast and on certain occasions you would remove it when you slipped into bed beside her oh so slowly so as not to wake her. So go, please, buck up and go. Right: and what if Alfredo opens the door for you? Try to imagine it, excuse me, an Alfredo maybe in his shorts, with a sleepy and irritated air who goes: Sorry, who are you? What do you want at this hour? What do you say to him: Biscou-Biscuit? Alfredo would whack you so hard it would send you tumbling down the stairs.

He got up and crushed the cigarette butt under his shoe. How strange, it seemed to him that the steps ringing out on the sidewalk were those of another. They were light, like someone following him. Who was following him? Oh, easy: it was that guy of many years ago who was following him, the same one who was no longer the same. And the hands too, he thought, how the hands change, how my hands have changed. Had they changed? Yes they had changed, as if the flesh that tapers the fingers and the soft cushion under the thumb had shifted to his belly, leaving his hands bony, almost skeletal. And speckled with a few liver spots. Which couldn't be seen now, because it was dark, but up there, once he went up, in the light, they would be seen clearly, too clearly. It's easy to say "go up." And what if there really was an Alfredo? You go up the little stairs ever so slowly counting to seven at every step. The seven plagues of Egypt, for seven years Jacob worked as a shepherd for Laban, seven years of misfortune, seven years of happiness, seven years of bad luck, seven deadly sins, seven-league boots, seven brides, seven brothers, from five to seven is the hour for lovers. But now it was half past midnight. Why had she taken her name off the doorbell? Maybe she didn't live here any more. Of course she lived here, it was a little typewritten label that had simply been ruined by the damp walls, and she had thrown it away. Go ahead, ring the bell, and about time too.

She was neither in her dressing gown nor in her night-gown. She was elegantly dressed, he thought, as if she had returned from a party or a dinner; he caught a glimpse of her though the chink in the door that the safety chain allowed. She merely asked him: What are you doing here, at this hour? What a fool, it was the only question he would never have thought she might ask him, the simplest, the one that you ask a friend whom you haven't seen for a week. Seven days, seven days had gone by, his reckoning had been wrong. It came to him like this: te voglio, te cerco, te chiammo, te veco, te sento, te sonno, he said quietly, without singing. What's that? She asked, Cchiù luntana me staie, cchiù vicina te sento, he continued. She slipped off the safety chain and opened the door. Come in, she said, I was about to go to bed. Have you eaten? He said: Yes, I mean no, I mean yes, a little bread and ham, but it's enough for me, I try to stay light evenings. I'll give you a piece of cake, she said, I'll get it from the kitchen, take a seat won't you?, I had guests this evening and I made the cake you like. Gâteau de la reine, he said, you made gâteau de la reine, goodness know how long it's been since I ate that. She came back with a tray. Because you're stupid, she said, I know very well how long it's been since you ate it, you don't know because you're stupid. She poured him a small glass of port. I've had the parquet redone, she said, do you like it? Nice, he said, shall we smoke a cigarette? I've quit, she said, bear with me, smoke it in peace, I'm going to bed, I'm a bit tired. May I come too? he asked.

Where does the geography of a woman begin? It begins with the hair, he answered himself. Do you know that the geography of a woman begins with her hair? he whispered in her ear. She was lying on one side and she turned her back to him. And then it continues with the nape and the shoulders, he said, all the way down to the bottom of the spinal column, this is where you enter the geography of a woman, for there, after the coccyx, there is a little lump of fat, or a little muscle like a chicken breast, and there the most secret zone begins, but first I need to caress your hair and then to tickle the nape of your neck ever so slowly; I came especially to tickle the nape of your neck, it seems to me that without your body my hands have lost their tactile sense, they have become ugly, dry and full of liver spots. You know I'm ticklish, she said, don't tickle me. Then I'll massage you, said he, I'll caress your shoulders as if I were gently massaging you, only with my fingertips. If you do that I'll fall asleep, she said, it's relaxing, bear with me. Sleep, he said, then I'll wake you, do you want me to sing you a *Lied* very softly? Are you still composing? she asked in a voice that was already drifting into sleep. Sometimes, he said, every now and again, but I have collected rather more than I have composed of late. How does that little song go that you recited to me as you came in? she asked. What little song? he said. The Neapolitan one, come on, don't pretend.

He continued to caress her with his right hand, and when with his left he passed over her body and touched her breasts, she was already asleep. He felt some small wrinkles, in her cleavage: the epidermis was creasing. But her breasts were still sweet, and warm, and the broad rosette around her nipples had lots of tiny pinpoints like seeds that wanted to sprout from beneath the earth. He thought how beautiful the geography of a woman was, and simple, if you know it and love it, and he thought that men are stupid, because they sometimes think they have forgotten it, and as he was thinking this he felt his body too beginning to breathe to the rhythm of the body he was embracing, and he thought: you must stay awake, wait, don't fall asleep now of all times.

When he reopened his eyes it was beginning to get light. In May dawn breaks early. In her sleep she had drawn up the blanket. Or perhaps he had done it, without realizing. He uncovered her and caressed her buttocks. Gently at first, then more forcefully, squeezing them. She moved in her sleep and let out a small muffled sound. You have a marvelous ass, it's one big smile, it's never tragic. She woke up. What's that you say? she asked. He repeated and then said: It's a poem. How silly you are! she said. With his left hand he groped for her sex. She clenched her legs. Recite me those verses you were reciting last night, she said, before I fell asleep. Which ones? he asked. The Neapolitan thing, she said, it was a song, I think. I don't remember it, he said. Sure you do, the one that went I want you, she said. Okay then, he said, it goes like this:

Sex contains all,
Bodies, Souls, meanings, proofs, purities, delicacies,
    results, promulgations,
Songs, commands, health, pride, the maternal mystery,
    the seminal milk;
All hopes, benefactions, bestowals,
All the passions, loves, beauties, delights of the earth,
All the governments, judges, gods, follow'd persons of
    the earth,
These are contain'd in sex, as parts of itself, and
    justifications of itself.

He said that caressing her pubis with his hand. You cheat, she said, that's Whitman. I want you, he said. Come in, she said. I'll do it like this, he said, from behind. No, she said, come on top of me, I want you to cover me. I didn't expect a word like that, on your lips, he said. It's a natural term, she said, it's a term of natural love. And she embraced him.

I'd like to sleep a bit more, he said, it's barely dawn. You were awake almost all night, she said, I heard you, you know. If I held you in my arms, will you get to sleep better? You know I will, he said. Do you want me to whisper something, she asked, once you would always ask me to talk, you fell asleep better. Whatever you like, he said. I know a Neapolitan song, she said, you know that I can't hold a tune very well, but I can try to sing it softly to you, it begins with I want you and ends with I dream of you.

Tell me: is this how it would be, if it were?

Letter to Write

A Letter is a joy of Earth –
It is denied the Gods

(EMILY DICKINSON, *Letters*)

My dear Woman,

I'd like to write you a letter, one day, a total letter, a true and total letter, I think about it, and I think about how it would be if I wrote it: it would be written with simple and recurrent words, used by all the people who have said them, and almost naïve, and vibrant with the passion of once upon a time. And passing through the obscure strata of lava and clay that life deposits over everything, it would tell you that I am still me, and that I still have dreams, except that I wake at dawn and sometimes my hand trembles when holding the pen or brush. And that the house is also the same: the old wood has the same smell and it allows the woodworm to gnaw at it; in summer a shaft of light comes in through the veranda window and on the opposite wall it traces Chinese shadows cast by the leaves of the vine that climbs up the railings, and then it is nice to stretch out on the wickerwork armchair, while outside, in the surrounding countryside, the noonday calm reigns and the crickets are not silent for one second; and they are without a doubt the same crickets, that is to say different and the same as ever. And that at the end of February, before sprouting leaves, the Japanese magnolia blooms again and it looks like a strange tub of flowers crystallized in the air, as if eternal. And, farther down the garden, the magnolia is joined by the mimosa you loved so much. And the children are growing too, exactly as before. Caterina is still on a diet, though with a certain reluctance, but she was really too chubby. At her age, however, she already has a sense of her own dignity and, as before, she is already flirtatious, and when she is grown up she will be a fascinating woman. Nino, on the contrary, is skinny as a beanpole and isn't doing too well at school, but it's because he doesn't apply himself, because his intelligence is already a foretaste of what he has become. And then I'd say that the evenings are long, terribly long, almost infinite, and languid, but that my heart reacts as it did before, and sometimes on hearing music, a sound, or a passing voice on the street, it begins to beat wildly, like a galloping horse. But, if the night wakes me, as ever, to calm that beating I get up and go to the living room; I light a yellow candle, because yellow is beautiful in the half light, and I read Sweet and clear is the night and without a breeze, and those words calm me, even though the wind outside shakes the branches of the trees and then I say to myself: Far from your branch poor frail leaf, where goest thou? I wonder about this and I try to get back to sleep and if I can't I poke the embers in the fireplace until they glow again a little, and in order to fall asleep I think that I'd write you that I didn't know that time doesn't wait, I really didn't know, we never think that time is made of drops, and you need only one drop more for the liquid to spill onto the floor and spread out like a stain before losing itself. And I'd tell you that I love you, that I still love, even though my senses seem tired, because they are, and that time, once so speedy and impatient, is now extremely slow in passing in certain hours of the afternoon, especially at the onset of winter, after the equinox when evening falls treacherously and the lights you weren't expecting are switched on in the village. And I'd also tell you that I have prepared the words for my tombstone, not very many, because between my date of birth and what will be my death all the days are mine, and I have had sufficient forethought to leave them to the little man who deals with these charitable services, by trade or by vocation. And then I'd tell you of that time when I saw you, as you were showing me the countryside, and that your petite figure outlined against the horizon struck me as the most beautiful thing the world had conceived, and I wanted to interrupt your erudite description by embracing you with the warmth of senses that were on fire. And then I would talk to you of certain nights in which we talked, of that house by the sea, of certain moments in Rome, of the Aniene, and of other rivers we have looked at together thinking that they flowed alone, without realizing that we were flowing along with them. And I would also tell you that I'm waiting for you, even though we don't wait for those who cannot return, because in order to go back to being who we were we would have to be who we were before, and that is impossible. But I'd say to you: Look, what has happened in all this time, which seems as impossible to pierce as a stratum of granite when the drill encounters it, well all this is nothing, it will definitely not prove an impossible obstacle to overcome when you read the letter I will write for you one day, you'll see, a letter I have always been thinking about, which has accompanied me all this time, a letter that I owe you and that I will really write, you can be sure of that, I promise you.

It's Getting Later All the Time

El candil se está apagando
la alcuza no tiene aceite . . .
No te digo que tu vayas
ni te digo que tu quedes. *

(Gypsy quatrain from Andalusia)

Avec le fil des jours pour unique voyage**

(JACQUES BREL, *The Flat Country*)

---

* The light is going out / the lamp has run out of oil . . . / I won't tell you to go /
nor will I tell you to stay.
** With the thread of the days, what a unique journey

Dear Sirs,

Despite the fact that this is a circular letter, our Company wishes to make it as personal as possible, not so much out of the hope of further relations between us, which as you will understand is impossible, as out of respect for that form of cordiality and civility that has characterized relations between us until now.

As you know, Dear Sirs, our Company boasts age-old experience. In the course of its business activities it has witnessed the most diverse vicissitudes, the greater part of which are unknown to all, although some of them will be perhaps known to you thanks to the echo, not infrequently exaggerated, given them by artists of all periods.

But troubles and complications are part of our profession: I would even say that such things sometimes offer us a break from the monotony and routine that is the usual lot of our Company. I presume, Dear Sirs, that you will already have had some experience of other companies, even simpler than ours, for example those firms that hire out means of locomotion. By contract, these firms make provision for accidents, covering them with insurance. Nonetheless there are some contingencies that no insurance company in the world can cover for the simple reason that a contingency, per se, appertains to the contingent. Let me offer an extremely banal example: a flat tire. A clause in the contract provides for appropriate and rapid assistance. But tires are not always punctured in circumstances that allow for appropriate or speedy assistance. You might try to imagine an ordinary Client driving a car along a cliff road that skirts a sheer drop down to the sea. The road is an endless series of bends, and dusk is falling. The unfortunate Client realizes that he has a flat right in the middle of a murderous hairpin bend, where, were a SUV to come along driven by certain impatient young-sters (this can happen, and that is what he is thinking) then there would be a crash before you could say knife. The Client, whose anxiety level has risen by several degrees, rummages in the trunk for the means of his salvation, the reflector triangle that might help him avoid a fatal accident. But he can't find it. Why? Because, while cleaning the car for the next client, some associate (they're always called associates, in those com-panies) forgot to put the reflector triangle back in its place. In the poor light of approaching evening, the Client, whose agi-tation is by this time at its peak, barely manages to read the instructions to be followed "in case of necessity" printed in the brochure issued by the rental car agency. Luckily (so he believes, the poor soul) there is a toll-free number for emer-gencies, and equally luckily he has a cell phone, bought in obedience to his wife's advice in anticipation of his journey abroad. He punches in the number, but, goodness gracious, the line is continually busy. Until . . . Oh, finally, it's ringing . . . but unfortunately by that time nobody is answering any more. Perhaps this story might strike you all as foolish, Dear Sirs, but I can assure you that for the hapless Client of whom I'm speaking this is a dramatic moment in his life. He will always remember a terrible moment in which night was falling over an unknown cliff and his car, which had a flat tire on a hairpin bend, where he risked being wrecked by a SUV driven by foolhardy youths, or, even worse, pulverized by some mammoth rig driven by a sleepy and maybe even drunk-en trucker.

I wouldn't like you to think, Dear Sirs, that with the example I have just quoted I wish put the understandable anxiety of the above-mentioned Client on the same level as the difficulties about which you have kept this Company informed during our long relationship. Comparisons between one client and another are always carefully avoided by this Company, for which I am in charge of contract termination. Contracts whose validity you might challenge with the objection that you did not sign them in your own hand. Alas, the fact is that your mere presence in this world, Dear Sirs, means that you have signed a contract: it consists of being born. And living. And, naturally, dying too. As I was saying about comparisons, it's better to avoid them. Largely because, each in his own way, in life, has tried to free himself of a thread or a wire, be it barbed or otherwise. And how many journeys have not been made in the company of someone only to realize in the end that we are alone? And let's not talk about mental labyrinths in which we think we relive as ours a time that was ours ·but is already no longer ours. And wanting to teach Sappho anacreontic meter is foolishness, believe me. You can understand the bacchanals, when the priest goes into ecstasies and the music of the cymbals and the tambourines breaks all meters to become obsessive, penetrating the gall bladder, from which it diffuses black melancholy and a nocturnal view of the universe: but trusting in melodramas that call for music worthy of a triclinium steeped in cheap perfumes strikes this Company as excessive and without a doubt unseemly. Besides, for some time we have known how the blood nourishes the atoms of men, and how it can steal the nourishment from them: we're sorry about that. And we have taken long walks too, we assure you: strolls that can even last a whole lifetime, but what does the algorithm of a life add to the infinite algorithm of a Company like ours? And again, the same thing seen from two different standpoints: doesn't that strike you as a bit boring? Come now! The universe is made of infinite points, and two miserable points of view are really not many. And if silence is really golden, why on earth write what had never been written or make the journey that had never been made? Do you not think, Sirs, that this is a form of craven capitulation?

You, Dear Sirs, are people who suffer, or at least people whom life has caused much suffering. This is plausible, and in cases like yours, in which on account of a choice that does not depend on our Company but on an unknown date that belongs to a higher office than ours, known as Expiry, we hold in store, quite exceptionally, a letter, which serves us almost as a brochure. It was written by a woman who was very dear to us and in certain special cases we send it to clients of the male gender like you, not only to alleviate your suffering, but also to remind you, albeit in the form of another circular, that recipients, whom you don't seem to have worried about thus far, have the right to be senders in their turn. This letter is not signed, Sirs, but it won't cost you much of an effort to work out who wrote it. Even though it had no title, my Sisters and I have called it *Letter to the Wind*. Our Company would be grateful if you would give it the attention it deserves.

Letter to the Wind

"*I disembarked on this island in the late afternoon. From the ferry I could see the little harbor coming closer, and the little white town nestling around the Venetian castle and I thought: maybe he's here. And as I walked through the lanes whose steps led up to the tower, with my baggage that was getting lighter every day, at every step I repeated: maybe he's here. In the little square beneath the castle, a terraced area overlooking the harbor, there is a typical local restaurant, with old iron tables along a low wall, two flower beds with two olive trees and bright red geraniums in rectangular tubs. Some old men*

*sit on the wall talking quietly, children run around a marble
bust of a mustachioed captain who was a hero of the Balkan
wars of the twenties. I took a seat at a table, set my baggage
down on the ground and ordered the specialty of the island,
rabbit with onions flavored with cinnamon. The first tourists
show up: it's the beginning of June. Night was falling, a transparent night that transformed the cobalt blue of the sky into
a bright violet, followed by darkness with a lingering trace of
indigo. On the sea glittered the lights of Paros, which seemed
a stone's throw away. Yesterday on Paros I met a doctor. He
hailed from the south, from Crete, I think, even though I did-
n't ask him. He's a short, robust man, with little broken cap-
illaries on his nose. I was looking at the horizon and he asked
me if I was looking at the horizon. I'm looking at the horizon,
I replied. The only line that breaks the horizon is the rainbow,
he said, the trickery of an optical reflection, pure illusion. And
we talked about illusions, and, without meaning to, I talked
about you. I mentioned your name without mentioning it,
and he said that he had known you because he had sutured
your veins the day you slashed your wrists. I didn't know
that, and it moved me, and I thought that in him I might have
found a bit of you, because he had known your blood. So I
followed him to his boarding house; it was called Thalassa,
and in fact it was on the seafront, and it was squalid, occupied by lower middle class Germans who come to spend their
vacations in Greece and who detest the Greeks. But he was-
n't like the Germans, he was kind; he undressed bashfully, and
he had a small penis, a bit crooked, like certain statues of
satyrs in terracotta in the Athens Museum. And he didn't so
much want a woman as some words of comfort, because he
was unhappy, and I pretended to give him some, out of
human compassion.*

*I have sought you, my love, in every atom of yours that is
dispersed in the universe. I have gathered as many as possible,*

in the land, in the air, in the sea, in the looks and gestures of men. I have sought you even in the kouroi, on a distant mountain on one of these islands, only because you once told me you had sat on the lap of a kouros. The ascent was not easy. The bus dropped me at Sypouros, which was the name of this village unknown on maps, and then I had to do over a mile on foot. I slowly made my way up the winding dirt track that farther on descends toward a valley with olive and cypress trees. There was an old shepherd along the way, and all I said to him was the only word that mattered: kouros. And in his eyes there glittered a light of complicity as if he had understood, as if he knew who I was and whom I was searching for, that I was searching for you, and without saying a word he stretched out his hand to show me the way, and I picked up the gesture with which he guided me and the light that had shone in his eyes for an instant and I put them in my pocket. Look, I have them here, I could lay them out on this table on this terrace where I am having dinner; they are another two fragments of this shattered fresco that I am desperately collecting in order to reconstruct you, beyond the odor of the man with whom I spent the night, the rainbow on the horizon and this azure sea that distresses me. But above all a barred window I found on Santorini, on which a vine climbed, and from which you could see the vastness of the sea and a little square. The sea was an infinity of square miles, and the square a handful of square yards, and in the meantime I recalled poems that talk of seas and squares, a sea of scintillating tiles that I once saw with you from a cemetery, and a little square where the locals had seen your face, and so mentally I sought you in the glittering of that sea because you had seen it, and in the eyes of the man in the village shop, the pharmacist, and the little old man who sold iced coffee in that square, because they had seen you. These things too I put in my pocket, in this pocket that is none other than myself and my eyes.

An Orthodox priest came out into the churchyard. He was sweating in his black vestments as he recited a Byzantine prayer in which the kyrie had your color. There is a boat on the horizon that leaves a streak of white foam on the blue. Is that you too? Maybe. I could put it in my pocket. But in the meantime a premature foreign tourist, premature as far as the season goes, because her age is almost venerable, is standing at the phone booth open to the wind and the passersby, facing the sea, and she says: Here the Spring is wonderful. I will remain very well. This is an expression of yours, I recognize it even when said in a foreign language, but in this case it is only a rough English translation of what you have already said, we know that well. Spring has passed for us, my dear friend, my dear love. And Autumn has already come, with the present yellow of its leaves. Let's even say that it is the depths of Winter in this early summer cooled by the breeze that blows this evening through the terrace overlooking the port of Naxos.

Windows: that's what we need, a wise old man in a distant land once told me, the immensity of the real is incomprehensible, to understand it you need to enclose it within a rectangle; geometry opposes chaos, that's why men invented geometrical windows, and every geometry presupposes right angles. Can it be that our life is also subordinated to right angles? You know, those difficult itineraries, made of segments, which we must all follow simply to reach our end. Perhaps, but if a woman like me thinks about this on an open terrace overlooking the Aegean Sea, on an evening like this, she understands that all that we think, live, have lived, imagine, and desire cannot be governed by geometry. And that windows are merely a timorous form of the geometry of men who fear the circular glance, where everything gains entry, without sense and without remedy, as when Thales looked at the stars, which do not fit in the frame of the window.

I have gathered all of you: crumbs, fragments, dust, traces, suppositions, accents lingering in the voices of others, a few grains of sand, a seashell, our past imagined by me, our supposed future, what I would have liked from you, what you had promised me, my childish dreams, the love that I felt as a girl for my father, some foolish rhymes from my youth, a poppy on the edge of a dusty road. I put that in my pocket too, you know? The corolla of a poppy like those poppies I went to pick on the hills in May with my Volkswagen, while you stayed at home full of your plans, devoting yourself to the complicated recipes that your mother had left you in a little black book written in French. And I was gathering poppies for you that you couldn't understand. I don't know if you put your seed in me or vice-versa. But no, no seed of ours ever bloomed. Everyone is only herself, without the transmission of future flesh, especially me without someone to gather my anguish. I have traveled around all these islands, all of them, in search of you. And this is the last island, as I am the last woman. After me, that's it. Who could carry on looking for you, apart from me?

You cannot betray me like this, cutting and running. Without my even knowing where your body lies. You handed yourself over to your Minos, whom you thought you had fooled but who in the end swallowed you up. And so I deciphered the epitaphs in all the cemeteries I could, in search of your beloved name, where at least I could weep for you. Twice you betrayed me, and the second time was by concealing your body from me. And now I am here, sitting at a table on this terrace, looking vainly at the sea and eating rabbit flavored with cinnamon. An indolent old Greek is singing an ancient mendicants' song. There are cats, children, two English people my age talking of Virginia Woolf and, in the distance, a lighthouse that they have not noticed. I had you find your way out of a labyrinth, and you had me go into one without there being any way out for me, not even the ultimate one. For my life has passed, and everything eludes me without the possibility of any link that might lead me back to myself or to the cosmos. I am here, the breeze caresses my hair and I am floundering in the night, because I have lost my thread, the one I gave you, Theseus."

Unfortunately, the time at our disposition is up. Clotho and Lachesis have completed their task, and now it's my turn. You, Sirs, will forgive me, but in this moment, which I am measuring with an hourglass different from yours, there has appeared for all of you the same year, the same month, the same day, and the same hour in which to cut the thread. And it is this that, not without displeasure, believe me, I am charged with doing. Now. At once. Immediately.

Postscript

If I remember aright, I began to write this novel in the form of letters around the autumn equinox of 1995. At that time I was especially interested in Sadeq Hedayat and the way he committed suicide in Paris, in the circulation of the blood as Andrea Cesalpino studied it in Pisa in the mid-16th century, in the workings of serotonin, in pain thresholds, and in friendships I thought were defunct and perhaps weren't.

At first it manifests itself as a trick of the memory with the letter here titled "Forbidden Games," first published as an introduction, in English and Portuguese, written to accompany a volume of pictures by the Brazilian photographer Márcio Scavone: *And Between Shadow and Light / E entre a sombre e a luz*, Dórea Books and Art, São Paolo 1997, later published in Italian with the title *Lettera a una Signora di Parigi*, in "La rassegna lucchese," n° 2, 2000. I say "a trick of the memory" because among Scavone's photographs there was a shot from the sixties in which a naked woman appears on a balcony stretching her arms out toward the sky, as if to embrace the air. And that image touched the memory of a Me so remote in time (and consequently so remote from the Me who looked at the photograph) as to make me think it was possible to attribute the memory of that image to a Me who was only a semblance, an ectoplasm of me lost in time. In short, a virtual stranger who was writing a letter.

The letter is an equivocal messenger. At least once in our life we have all received a letter that seemed to come from an imaginary universe, when instead it really existed in the mind of whoever wrote it. And probably we have sent similar missives ourselves, perhaps without realizing that we were entering a space that is real for us but unreal for others, a reality of which the letter is moreover the most honest counterfeiter, because it fools us into thinking we can bridge the distance between us and the distant person. People are distant when they are at our side, never mind when they are really distant.

Sometimes we may have happened to write to ourselves. And I'm not talking about the fictions, the often sublime letters, of which certain writers of the past were capable: I'm talking about real letters, duly stamped and franked. Sometimes we may even write to the dead. It doesn't happen every day, I'll admit, but it can happen. And it may even be that the dead reply, in some form that only they know. But the most disquieting thing, which gnaws like stubborn woodworm ensconced in an old table and is impossible to silence without a poison that would poison us too, is the letter we never wrote. "That" letter. The one that all of us have thought of writing, on certain sleepless nights, and that we always put off until the following day.

If I were asked for an opinion about the nature of these letters transformed into a novel I wouldn't rule out the idea of describing them as love letters. In a very broad sense, as vast as the territory of love, which often encroaches upon unknown and apparently alien territories such as rancor, resentment, nostalgia, and regret. And in fact these are some of the places in which these characters, the senders of the letters that I set to writing, wander about as if lost. And, if not love, nonetheless something akin to a sorrowful affection inspires the last character, the only female voice in this book and one who spends her life snipping other people's lives with her shears.

I would like to talk about the whys and wherefores of

some of the letters, perhaps because every story always has a sub-story.

Suddenly, one summer, I thought I saw again a storm I had seen eighteen years before. Thinking you can relive the unrepeatable is a foolish idea, even though the external and internal circumstances strike us as identical and thus corroborate our illusion. The same constituent elements of that remote event were in fact present: the same vantage point (the window of an isolated inn), the same place observed (a landscape with rugged hills), the same air charged with electricity that was transmitted to the mind and the thoughts, the same moon scudding madly through inky clouds. I threw the window wide open, leant against the parapet and set to waiting patiently. In such circumstances it is necessary to light a cigarette, or a candle, and think of one's dead, as I had done many years before. I did that again, but the storm did not break, leaving the landscape motionless. Instead it broke in my head like a cosmic migraine that swelled the tides of blood in my cranium. And it exploded with the music of Bellini's *Norma*, which is pompous and arrogant music—like all the works of those fine artisans that consider themselves great artists—but in harmony with the abominable verses of Felice Romani's libretto. As a substitute for the storm that didn't come there sprang "Casta Diva," and I had the narrator conduct the orchestra of a disjointed and demented opera, as when the atmosphere is racked by the elements. And since that narrator presumed to arrive at the knowledge of a real event in the same way as a shaman who calls for the rain—that is to say by skipping the steps of substantial logic, by employing intuition and arbitrary choice, and recomposing the event to be understood according to a wholly personal logic—I concluded that that character was moving on a level of the logic of delirium. Perhaps he was mad. In the beginning of September, Ricardo Cruz-Filipe invited me to his home in Lisbon to see his latest paintings. For some time I had promised Cruz-Filipe a text about his work and I had never written it. That day, on looking at some pictures, and especially the *disiecta membra* of the "Caravaggioesque" ones, I clearly understood that I had *already* written that text. It was the piece I titled "Casta Diva." And I also understood that the madmen are not the shamans who dance so that the storm will break, but the phony meteorologists who announce that the storm forecast for today might not come for another two days. And why, besides? Simply because meteorologists want everything to happen in accordance with order and logic, and that morning may come to seal a night spent in the arms of Morpheus. And then on to rest in peace, in order to pick up that routine thanks to which a person knows that life is all here, and never elsewhere.

The letter titled "The River" was at first titled *Senza fine* ("Without End"), on thinking of an unforgettable work by the Italian singer-songwriter Gino Paoli, largely because it seemed to me that words like: "You are a moment without end, you have no yesterday, you have no tomorrow" cannot be said to a woman with impunity: they demand development, whatever it may be. It's not impossible that some might recall *A terceira margem do rio* by Guimarães Rosa, a story whose majesty impressed me as much as the sight of the Amazon River. But, as we have said, literature is not a train running along the surface, but a karsic river that emerges where it will, in the sense that its course eludes all surface surveillance. And then it ought to be added that Guimarães Rosa's river, immense though it was, possessed a third bank, while the river referred to in this story is devoid of banks. But perhaps it is not improbable that both stories have taken something from the banks of Plotinus's third *Ennead*, as Porphyry handed it down to us, where we read of an infinite river that is at once Beginning and Absence, primordial emanation and the impossibility of measurable definitions. But on mature reflection this account above all taps the life of its protagonist. For writers know the life of their characters really well, even in their deepest well-springs: and I do not say this out of arrogance, believe me. To those who, thanks to familiarity with narratology, this letter may appear "labyrinthine," I would like to point out that it was written in a place where the labyrinth is an ancient presence. To be precise in Haniá, in Doma, in the home of Ioanna and Rena Koutsoudaki. And to Ioanna and Rena, and to the memory of their peerless hospitality, it is affectionately dedicated. The letter also owes a debt to the friendship of Anteos Chrysostomidis, who one June Sunday in Crete had the patience to set down in a notebook many pages that, as I could not write them in person, I was obliged to "write" orally.

"I Dropped By to See You, But You Weren't Home" was written thinking about Robert Walser's "strolls," which lasted a lifetime, and the letter is dedicated to his memory. "Books Never Written, Journeys Never Made" was written on the train between Paris and Geneva, round trip. The French philosopher alluded to is Clément Rosset and the book in question is *Le reel, l'imaginaire e l'illusoire*. This text is dedicated to Jean-Marc, a Parisian *clochard* who has traveled the world without moving from his patch of sidewalk. "What's the Use of a Harp With Only One String?" owes much to the memory of a friend who departed one day for his own Elsewhere without coming back, to a brief encounter with the representative of the Jewish Community of Salonika, to the pianist Sandro Ivo Bartoli, with whom it is nice to talk about music, and to a person who once talked to me about Alexandria of the remote past. "Strange Way to Live" takes its title from an old *fado* by Amália Rodrigues, and can be read as a tribute to Enrique Vila-Matas and to the anthropophagic brilliance of his work. "On the Difficulty of Freeing

Oneself from Barbed Wire" can be considered a continuation of "Forbidden Games," or an appendix to it, almost as if the sender of those letters had realized that the recipient had not found his message in a bottle, and especially that *repetita non juvant*.

It's not worth talking about the other stories: they saw the light here and there, sometimes heard, sometimes imagined; other times they sprang from goodness knows where, at their whim. I only want to say that I lifted the letter within the letter, titled "Letter to the Wind," from a novel I have yet to write. If I write it one day I'll give it back. The letter within which it is included could well be considered my personal letter, that's for sure. For it seems right to me to silence one's own characters in the end, after having had the patience to listen to their querulous stories. It's a way of telling them that the time granted them is up and that they may not return to torment us with their presence. So, off you go.

T.

In passing this book on for publication my grateful thanks go to Veronica Noseda, who with affectionate friendship and enormous patience transformed the notebooks that contained this novel into a typescript, and to Massimo Marianetti, who transcribed the first texts.